Amani,

Follow your dreams!

T.H. Stickland

Sir Banion and the Quest of the Black Plague

By T. H. Strickland

Cover Art by Kimberly Stephens

ISBN: 978-1500483555
ISBN-13: 1500483559

thstrickland.com

PROLOGUE

The knight pitched forward after slipping in the mud and gasped as the chain fell out of his hands. His prisoners tumbled down after him snapping their jaws and wiggling towards him trying to bite him without the use of their hands.

The rain was pouring down steadily and the knight was quickly covered in mud and filth as he flailed around blindly trying to escape their reaching mouths. He wiped the muck off of his face and stepped away. He kicked at one that had gotten too close and received a dull moan in response.

It had taken him six days, most of which had been raining, to get this close to the coast. He had to take his prisoners to Ireland and could not get there soon enough. He hadn't slept in days, and there was a nagging fear that he would become the next victim of his prisoners' murderous intent. Their next meal. No one would find his body, and no one would ever know he was gone.

He had been away from home for the better part of a month on a quest for his father and the king. He wanted nothing more than to be back in England and not in this Godforsaken stretch of land in France. He would finish his mission in Ireland, and go home to a well-deserved rest. Well, actually, he would go home to prepare.

These would not be the last to cross the channel and he had to get ready to defend his land and his father's house. Hopefully, however, these were the first and he wasn't too late. A twig snapped behind him and he started with a jolt. He turned drawing his sword but nothing came out of the grey dark to face him. He knew his real enemy was tangled on the ground behind him.

He took a few deep breaths to calm himself and sheathed his sword. It would take him an hour to get them back up on their feet and walking again. Luckily, he had the perfect bait to keep them going. Himself. He was very careful as he found the end of the chain. He traced it with his eyes from one set of wrists, to the neck, and then to the next in line.

He was right. It did take him almost an hour slipping and struggling to get them all clear. He continued down the path dragging the chain behind him as he wrapped his cloak once again around his shoulders. In a few days more he would be in Ireland to begin the preparations. It was unlikely that any of them were ready for what he brought with him.

CHAPTER 1

I woke with a start just as the jaws of the monster closed around my neck. It was another nightmare about the unknown danger of the trials that I would face later today. The dreams had been coming for weeks, and my anxiety at the thought of what I would have to face was mounting. The truth was that I would not know what it meant to be a man until it was forced upon me.

It is my sixteenth birthday, the day that I am either to join the ranks of the proud knights of Ireland or forget all my dreams and all that I have been working on and start down a new path to some less glorious future. I've been looking forward to this day my entire life. Finally, it has arrived.

All my training and ceaseless work have brought me to this day. If all went according to plan at the trials this morning, then my father would grant my commission to travel to Dublin, to the table of my Uncle at the castle, and ask to be blessed in my knighthood. Of course, I had to make it through the trials first.

Many would assume that being the son of the King of Cork would be enough to pass the trials of knighthood, but this is not the case. Even my being the nephew of the High

King of Ireland was not enough anymore. Irish knights are held to such a standard that even a king's son could be denied the right to become a knight. I did not want to end up some knight's squire carrying around his lances and helping him put on his armor, or be some man at arms hoping for glory as I saw the knights ride by on their tall horses.

Of course, it was not always this way. There used to be no question that a king's son would be knighted. I am nobility after all. Things changed, though, when Arthur's bastard tried to overthrow the kingdom across the sea. Now, we have the trials.

The world was not the same as it once was. Arthur's court across the channel has fallen into shambles; Mordred, that swine-son, tore that great fellowship apart. Then Sir Mordred's body was found after the battle and the rumors tell that Arthur was killed as well. That country's future is still uncertain even now almost fifty years later. Maybe it is now time for Ireland to show her power. Rumors tell of a Norman invasion in the spring, but who can trust such hearsay. It is time to focus though.

I will have to prove that I am not only well trained in the warring arts, but that I am noble of mind as well. Some say that chivalry is a dead art. This is not true in Ireland, and this is why we host the greatest knights in the world. Not only are we victorious on the battlefield, but each one of us fight on the side of truth, goodness, king, and country.

I was not going to let failure happen to me though. I

have spent endless hours training for this very day. I'm sure even more than my fellows have trained. Sure, they are all of noble blood too, but that is not enough these days. The world is a dark place.

The trials start at eight which must be a few hours from now. I cannot sleep anymore, I'm too nervous. I will go to the great hall and see about breakfast. I cry out as I push the furs off of myself,
        "Come, Fang! You can't sleep all the time!"

Fang was who I could trust through it all. The most loyal beast a man could have. He is part wolf I think, from the north. I remember when my father gave him to me when he was a pup. He had found him on a hunting trip and brought him back to give to me. Father said he was born to be a killer. A devil of the north woods. A hell hound. I'm glad he is on my side. He even nips at the knights of my father's court. He has no fear.

I turned to the task at hand. Breakfast. The stone was cold on my bare feet. I danced across the floor trying not to touch the cold ground with my bare toes. It is with delight that I notice them next to the hearth. The servant must have put them there during the night while tending the fire. It is still rather drafty as I make my way downstairs. I hear voices coming from the great hall as I open the door. The knights have gathered early in preparation for the trials.

I overhear one of my father's knights, Sir Gareth, as I pass.
"Look who has risen early this marnin'," said Sir Gareth.

"Young Master Banion."

He was answered by another knight, "He was probably too scared to sleep with the trials today, Sir Gareth."

"Very funny," I replied. "What wakes you up so early Gareth? The itch make it hard to sleep?"

I spoke boldly and perhaps a little stupidly. Sir Gareth stood up at this and reached for his ax. Right as he stood, a dagger hit the bench between his legs and silenced his anger as he cried out in shock and surprise.

"What's wrong Sir Gareth, a little shy about that itch? Maybe spend some time bathing and your beard wouldn't be so appealing to bugs"

I see that the speaker is Sir Jahnis as he walked confidently across the room towards us. Sir Jahnis was my father's sergeant at arms and he was known to be a confident and superb soldier. His reputation alone was able to keep Sir Gareth from slapping me around just hours before the trials.

"Come along Master Banion. I want to talk to you about something" said Sir Jahnis.

I quickly went to Sir Jahnis' side and walked with him to a bench at the back of the hall. He motioned for food to be brought to us and a servant quickly came with heaping plates of sausages, bacon, eggs, mushrooms, and beans. Luckily, my nervousness did not affect my appetite. I tore ravenously into the food. Slyly, I slipped some sausage to

Fang under the table. Fang kept giving Sir Gareth a mean look and I would have to say that Sir Gareth was quite lucky to have quieted when he did or Fang might have had a thing or two to discuss with him on my behalf.

Sir Jahnis sat quietly looking at me. I wondered if he was ever going to start speaking. The quiet was too intense, I have to say something. "Um, thanks Jahnis…"

He cut me off, "No need lad, Gareth is a flea. But, I have to say he is quite the loyal flea at that, and that is a good quality in a man and in a soldier. He just needs to be reminded now and again of his manners.

I want to speak to you about something, though," continued Sir Jahnis. "How do you feel about today and the trials?"

I answered quickly, "You have trained me well Sir Jahnis, and I fear nothing that I will face today. I know of no way that I could possibly be better prepared."

Jahnis smirked as if he expected such a practiced and courteous answer. He answered, "Do you know what hubris is Banion?" I stared down at the bacon on my plate and wondered what answer he was looking for. "Well," I spoke, "I remember the lessons, it's Greek or something." Maybe I hadn't focused on my studies enough, would they challenge my knowledge at the trials? Was Jahnis testing me or letting me in on a secret?

"Greek, huh? Yes. But what does it mean?" asked Sir

Jahnis. He answered his own question without waiting, "It means excessive pride, lad. It leads to the downfall of many a hero in the past. I bring it up because I do not want you to fall to the same fate. You have a good head on your shoulders and you are strong at arm, but remember the Lord Jesu has given you these gifts and you must not forget thanks."

"But," I interrupted.

"Listen," said Jahnis. "You are well trained, but so is everyone else. Do not think the others have not been training constantly as well. Remember that you will only be sent to Dublin if you are worthy. Trust me; we know when a man is worthy. Today's trials are going to be different than any before, so don't let your pride get the best of you. Remember it is better to go slow and watch what is happening before rushing into battle. See what your battle is before you fight it. I do not fear for you, Banion, but keep your head on your shoulders and remember what I have told you today."

At these words Sir Jahnis stood and left me to ponder the words he had hastily given me. What did pride have to do with anything? Weren't we supposed to be proud men? I was confused. I feel like he spent years teaching me to be proud and then just told me, the day of the trials I might add, that I shouldn't be proud. Now I am worried. Fang nipped at my ankle under the table, I had neglected to give him anything off my plate in my distraction and he can be so impatient. "Such a selfish animal," I jokingly thought. I would need his strength and courage today though.

By this time, the hall had begun to fill up. I saw Sir Jahnis go over and fetch his dagger from Sir Gareth. He said something and they all laughed. I wonder what he said to them. I saw my contemporaries come in with their fathers. They looked as nervous as I felt; that must be a good sign. There were fifteen of us being tested today. I wonder how many will make it? It was not uncommon for a man to be killed or maimed at the trials and forever be shamed by their lack of fortitude. As I got up and made my way across the hall I was hailed by many a knight that wished me luck in the trials. As if luck was enough. I hope I can stand up to how they think I should do.

CHAPTER 2

It was getting late and as I walked out of the hall a servant met me in the corridor.

"Master Banion, the king wishes to see you before the trials," He said. "Very well," I responded. "I will see him now."

I followed the servant to my father's receiving chambers and was announced upon my entry. My father sat on the other side of the room, an impressive figure, and Sir Jahnis stood at his side. My father and uncle were not handed their kingdoms. They fought a long and hard war against the corrupt monarchy that had ruled Ireland for almost a century and even battled the English on a whim and with no wrong done against them.

The years of fighting could be seen on my father's face. He had a long scar down the left side where his reign had almost ended before it started. A lucky strike from an enemy sword as my father fought alone in the middle of the battlefield cut off from his brother and the rest of their forces. The legends tell that he killed three score men that day all alone. As I walked in he dismissed all the courtiers and I was left alone with him and Sir Jahnis.

"Banion, my boy. Come to me." My father said.

As I walked towards him he leaned towards Sir Jahnis and the two spoke. As I approached I could see the look of approval on my father's face. I had hit my growth spurt later than the other boys my age and my father had wondered if I would become a warrior like himself. He was very pleased that I had shot up eight inches and gained thirty pounds of muscle in the last year and a half.

"You see, Sir Jahnis" the king said, "A strong boy we have here, one who will make a fine King one day."

Sir Jahnis answered, "Lucky to have a son of such a sound mind as well as a warrior's body, my king."

"Banion, tell me of the trials. Do you feel fully prepared me boy?" I stood up straight as I responded, "Sir Jahnis has trained me well, father, I fear nothing on the battlefield, but I do fear the unknown; what will I have to face today?"

"Ah," he said. "Even the King's son cannot know what he will face before he faces it. It would not be a fair test if one knew more than the others, but I can tell you that there is a new element, a fascinating one indeed that no one has had to face ever before. It will take all your training and your intellect to beat such a foe." I thought about his words coupled with Sir Jahnis' warning minutes before about remembering to use my mind, not be prideful, and know what I was getting into before I rushed in.

My father continued, "Sir Jahnis has told me much of your training and aptitude. We do not fear for you, son, but wish you well in the trails. It is your destiny to one day rule the Southern Kingdom and this is just one step further on that path. Before you go, prepare yourself, I wanted to give you a gift.

As you know, each competitor in the trials is allowed the weapon of their choice but at your age none of your contemporaries or you has been given a weapon to call your own. You are just allowed to train with all types so that you will know where your skill lies."

I wondered what he was getting at as he continued. "I was very glad to hear from Sir Jahnis that you have particular skill with a sword. Maybe even beyond a normal man's ability. He tells me that given time and training you can be one of the best swordsmen that have ever graced this hall, even better than your old da. Well, given that I can only give you one item to take with you I will give you the best I can."

My father nodded to Sir Jahnis who reached behind my father's chair and brought out a long object wrapped in cloth. It had to be a sword; my father was giving me a sword for the trials! I thought that most boys were just allowed to take a weapon out of the armory for use in the trial but this was beyond my wildest dreams. The trials were so secretive. No one knows what happens in them except the knights who make it through them, and they are sworn to secrecy on their lives.

Every three years when the trials are held, the whole castle waits forever for the results to be announced. Some families cheer to hear that their sons have made it, and some drop in misery to find their sons had been injured or killed. There are rumors that those who are too grievously injured to become knights are given the opportunity to die an honorable death instead of becoming a squire or a servant. Some accept such news as their fate and stoically take up that mantle.

My father beckoned me forward and I started to unwrap his gift. I knew I was right as a hilt peaked out from under the wrappings. It was a sword.

"This was the sword my father gave me when I was going to war and it was the sword his father gave him. One day, I hope you can give it to your son. Its name is Oíche which means "night" in the old language and it will serve you well until you are ready to let it rest before passing it on to your son.

I could not remove my eyes from the sword and I wondered how long my father had used this sword. It was not the sword he carried on his side now, and it was not the one he had warred with. So, I asked, "father, how long did you use Oíche?"

"Ah," He answered, "this sword was too off for my tastes my lad; I needed a little longer sword with more weight behind it to hack my enemies to pieces! Haha! But, I bet it is perfect for you…"

I finished unwrapping the sword and pulled out a beautiful weapon. I lost the ability to speak in its presence. The blade was long, it was made out of black onyx, not metal, and there was a slight curve to the blade. It had a strong steel cross piece and the handle had grooves for my fingers. The pommel was adorned with a single garnet stone in the end which reflected in the light as my father handed me the sword. I expected the weapon to be very heavy because the blade was made out of stone, but it felt perfect. My hand fit the sword as if it was made for it and it was perfectly balanced.

"Go ahead, boy, swing it around a bit and get a feel for it" the king said.

I stepped back, spread my feet into my fighting stance and prepared the sword. It felt perfect, I started to swing the sword around my head and I slashed down in front of me, I jabbed and stabbed and blocked my imaginary opponent and it felt as if Oíche was reading my thoughts and was making the moves before my mind told my body to do it. I had never felt so connected to a weapon before, I spun across the room, sidestepped, danced, kicked, and blocked.

As I finished my steps I came across the room and slashed downwards, as if not on purpose, on the grand table in my father's room. The table was huge and oak, weighing hundreds of pounds, and I slashed straight through it to the ground and cut a huge gash in the stone floor. As I quickly turned in disbelief to apologize to my father I heard him laugh and saw him jump to his feet.

"Did you see that Jahnis, right through the table into the floor!" My boy that sword was made for you! I never was able to do such a thing with it.

Sir Jahnis stepped to my side and said with a smile, "Banion, it is very lucky for you to find a weapon so suited to you this early in your life. Some men live their entire lives fighting with something they feel no connection to." He took the sword from me, put it in its scabbard, and fit the scabbard to my waist. "You are now ready for all that comes your way, but remember what I said earlier." He then stepped away and left the room after bowing to my father.

My father came up to me. "Banion, you have made your father very proud. I am glad to have you as my son. I wish you luck in the trials. Keep your head about you, and don't be too hasty in anything we put in front of you. Now go and make any last preparations you need to."

I left his chambers and met Fang in the hall; I knelt and showed him Oíche. He sniffed the sword, and then barked as if in approval. It was almost time. We must go meet the rest of the boys in the great hall.

CHAPTER 3

I went down the stairs with Fang at my heels. I wanted to find my best friend, Sean, and show him my sword before the trials. Sean was the son of one of my father's best knights and we had grown up in the castle together. We had been born two weeks apart in the depths of a terrible blizzard in January. Our fathers always said that surviving the blizzard was what had made us so strong and since we had survived it together, we had become best friends.

The only difference between Sean and I was that Sean was huge. I stood at six feet high and I weighed one hundred and eighty pounds. No small man indeed, but Sean, Sean was easily six foot five inches tall and two hundred and thirty pounds of muscle. He had even been wrestling and sparring with some of the older knights because he was so big and naturally a fighter. He was going through the trials today as well.

As I came to the bottom of the stairs I saw Sean coming towards me with a huge smile on his face. He held his hand behind his back and I knew that his father must have given him a weapon as well. I could see part of the haft behind his back which can only mean he was given a big weapon indeed.

"Banion!" he said as we embraced. "Take a look at this!" Out from behind his back he pulled out a huge hammer. The staff was half as long as his body, a hard wood that had rings of steel burnt into the wood to give it strength. On the end of the staff was another foot of hard steel ending in a hammer head that was a hard ball of steel on one side, and a pointed spike on the other. This weapon was made to break bones and crush skulls. "Sean!" I said, "What a hammer!"

Sean began to tell me the story as he handed me the hammer. He said, "My father had it made for me, using my dimensions to make it perfect for me. It feels so good in my hands, Banion, I have never been more confident in a weapon. But what about you, did your dad give you a..."

He gasped as I pulled Oíche out of the sheath and presented him the hilt. Sean took the sword in his hand and briefly forgot his hammer as he marveled at my new sword. His hammer was heavy, I couldn't imagine swinging this in battle, but I bet Sean will use it so naturally. "What an amazing sword," he said. Your skill with the blade will be even greater with a weapon such as this.

"And this impressive hammer," I said. "What can stand in our way with these?" We switched back our weapons and Sean grasped my arm tightly. "No matter what happens today," he said. "We do this together; nothing can stand in our way!" I smiled; with a friend such as this the worry of the trials began to fade.

Suddenly, those fears came rushing back as the King called from the top of the stairs. "Gather all!" he boomed loudly.

The crowd came in, noblemen and ladies, sons and daughters. The whole castle gathered to hear what he had to say. Sean and I stood off to the side and looked at the other boys who would be fighting for their manhood today. There were fifteen in all including Sean and I. Many of them stood with their families, with their mothers clutching their arms, and their fathers remembering their own challenge at the trials and placing that reassuring hand on their son's shoulders.

There would be none of that for Sean and I. Sean's mother had died during his birth, and my mother had become sick when I was a mere infant and passed away. We had been raised by the same nurse, Ann, and this probably contributed to how we were practically brothers. Sean's father stood near mine at the top of the stairs. Our fathers had shown their support of us in private and we now needed only our companionship to have courage; we did not need a parent's coddling.

The king began to speak again. "Noblemen, ladies, friends, and neighbors, It is a great thing when a boy becomes a man, but it is no easy feat. The trials have been in place for a hundred years; the purpose is to show who the best of Ireland's men are, and to show us the pride of our people. Ireland calls only its best to become knights and because of that I salute my fellow knights in this room today. Slainté!"

Knights all over the room called out in response to my father's words. It was a huge honor to be called a knight in our country. "Today we call our sons to step forward and take their place among us. There are fifteen who strive to be our equals. We honor them and wish them well! Slainté!"

The knights all called out luck to us.

"Mothers say goodbye to your sons, fathers wish them well. You have armed them and trained them. It is time to see what they have learned. We meet at the proving grounds in one hour; knights take your sons on horseback by the trial road and then join me in the observation area." The king said. There was a hustling and bustling within the crowd as the echoes of his words died out.

My father came down the stairs with Sir Jahnis and Sean's father, Sir Bower. Sir Jahnis shook my hand, then Sean's, and walked out the castle door and down to his horse. I guess he has preparations to do for the trials. My father clasped me on the back and walked me out the front door to the stables.

"Lad, there is nothing more I can teach you" he said as we mounted our horses. We started to ride out the gate and down the hill towards the black forest. "There are many things that we do not tell outsiders, and there are things we do not tell our wives or children, but when a son comes of age he is granted such knowledge. The world is a dark place. More than most people know or experience in the safety of the castle walls. Your uncle and I have fought to make Ireland a better place, but the evil of the world is relentless."

He paused as we passed under the trees before continuing, "God blesses us with the discernment of good and evil. We are knights of good, but that is not the case for all. I wish I could tell you that all fifteen of you boys would make it today, but not all of you will. Some of you will become injured, some will decide they do not want to be warriors, and some may even perish in the trials. Unfortunately, that is not the only options.

Some have had the skill to be a warrior, but we will judge them to not be worthy of being a knight of Ireland. If they have a black heart we cannot give them power. These men will leave in anger and exile themselves from our company. As they travel the world they will learn and brood and cause trouble for the good for the rest of their lives. That is the path they choose. It is then our duty to destroy them when they threaten the safety of our land and people. We cannot hesitate in our duty to this.

There is more to this than what I have said. A new evil has made it to our shores and it adds more danger to your life's purpose than you already would have had to deal with. I cannot explain it all to you now, but it is like a plague and it is burning its way across Europe.Before it reaches Ireland's shores we need to know as much about it as we can. I know I am being vague, but you will understand of what I speak soon enough. Just remember what Sir Jahnis has told you, remember your training, and always take strategy over haste. You must know your enemy before you can defeat it."

These words my father said were disheartening. There was evil in the world, and the unknown. What danger were we going to have to face? As my father spoke we passed into the woods and were riding on a dark road into the deep forest. The path became narrow and I allowed my horse to fall in line behind his. I could hear horses in front of and behind us and I guessed that these were my fellows and their fathers. Were they getting the same news as I?

We rode for another forty minutes into the woods and then came upon a large gate flanked by two of my father's guards. They saluted as we passed under the gate, and we came upon a large clearing. We were not the first there and we dismounted and tied our horses to a post. The knights and their sons were gathered in small groups and everyone was talking in a tense readiness. Sean and his father rode in not long after we had and they joined us. Within ten minutes, the last of the fifteen competitors and their fathers came in and gathered together.

Sir Jahnis came out of a gate on the other side of the clearing and whispered something to my father.

"Good, good." The king said. He then addressed the gathered crowd. "Knights, you may take your places in the observation area of the grounds. Boys, there is much to tell about how the trials work so listen up. The trials will test you over every aspect of your abilities. There will be many of you who wish to not continue after certain tests. There is no shame in this. If you do not wish to continue you must present yourself to the knights and we will grant you permission to withdraw. You will then be allowed to watch the rest of the trials and you will be spoken to about what your next steps will be."

I looked sideways at Sean and saw a slight curve on the side of his mouth as he tried not to smile. This would not be us. The king finished, "But now, the time for banter is over. The time for proving has come. Luck to all of you lads, Sir Jahnis will lead you into trial grounds." With that my father left us. This was it. We were alone with just the skills and abilities we had harnessed up to this point in our lives. Would it be enough? I didn't know.

CHAPTER 4

Sir Jahnis came up to the group of boys as the other knights began to disappear into the trees around us. He beckoned for us to follow him without saying another word. The group shifted awkwardly as we began to follow his lead. Sean stepped up to my side and I looked and saw a confident smirk on his face. He nodded to me without saying a word. I smiled back; no fear, we were in this together. I looked behind me and caught the eye of our friend, Edward, and gave him a nod. The three of us had been training together for as long as we could remember and our friendship was rock solid.

As we began to walk up the trail we came to a split with three forks in the road. Sir Jahnis stopped and separated the large group into three groups of five and then told us to continue down whatever path he had placed us on. Sean and I ended up in the same group and Edward was with us too. I felt safer with them at my side since Fang was not allowed to come to the trials. I bet he was tearing my room to pieces for being trapped in the castle.

Sir Jahnis left with the group to the left and another knight stepped up to lead my group down the path to the right. I had never seen him before but he was different. He had a lean look and he shifted uneasily as twigs would snap or the wind would shift the trees around us. I wonder what he has seen in his life to make him so uncomfortable in the woods. He had to be a proven fighter or he would not be given such an important task as a facilitator for the trials. This was a weird observation for me of the man to say the least.

We came to a clearing and I quickly looked around to see what we were to face but the only thing in the clearing was a large round table with five seats at it. The anxious knight informed us to take a seat and then moved to the outer circle of the clearing where he seemed to be keeping a careful watch on the outside of the circle at the woods around us. In the dark canopy above I could hear the shifting of armor and mail. There must be catwalks up above where our fathers and the other knights would watch the trials.

We took our places at the table as an old knight came down the path and looked us over. I had seen him before at my father's table usually when the trials were about to begin. He was of my uncle's house I believe, and had been facilitating the trials for years.

He spoke in a tired and raspy voice: "lads, this exercise will test your intellect and your eye for strategy. Each one of you will be given a situation and your known forces, and then you will have an hour to write out your strategy for overcoming your obstacles. You may not consult one another. Your actions and the actions of the men you have under your command will be judged."

"Strategy?" Sean said. "Not exactly my strong suit.

Actually, writing is not my strong suit. I can think of some strategy but putting it into words will not be easy." Sean laughed a little, but I could see some concern on his face as well. He wasn't happy at what we were about to do. Sean was a natural fighter, and with his big build and strength he could best most opponents. He can read his opponent and always be two steps ahead in a battle. This is only in battle though.

Sean is perfectly willing to have someone else tell him where to battle and then do it better than anyone else. He looked worried. I wasn't too confident myself but I guess I will have to see. The facilitator called for silence as we had took our seats. The old knight continued after we were seated, "You have an hour. You will be given a break halfway through your time." Parchment was passed out as well as quills and ink. In front of each one of us was a scroll that was bound in a red ribbon. The facilitator called for us to start and I opened mine. It said:

You command a small scouting party of 16 men.
Seven archers
Seven Swordsmen
Your Lieutenant
And yourself.
You are all on horseback.
It is early morning as you come through the woods and you are met by a young boy who is running as if for his life. You dismount and he tells you that he has just escaped from a slave camp and has been running for an hour. He tells you that the slavers are hard men who spoke a strange language. They have been stealing

young boys and girls all over the country and have eight captives. The boy cannot tell you an exact number of the enemy, but he thinks there are at least twice your number of slavers. He also says that groups of five or so of them will be gone off raiding at one time, and they can come back at any time. Surely, they will have noticed the boy has left and have sent a search party after him. The boy has hardly been fed and can barely stand any longer. What do you do?

My first thought was to rush to find the slavers and attack. This would be rash though. The advice of my father and Sir Jahnis came into my head. I knew that I had to think strategically. It was never as easy as we think it should be. I looked over at Sean, and saw that he was deep in concentration, but looked very confused. I suppressed a smile. This should be easy. Think. I began to write:

First: All soldiers dismount. Give the boy food, a blanket, and water and assure him of his safety.

Second: All swordsmen spread out to make a perimeter so that our camp is safe at a distance of one hundred yards out and twenty yards in between each swordsman in a circle around the camp.

Third: Send out the archers. They can move quietly without being noticed and cover more ground more quickly than the soldiers in armor with swords. They can go in groups of two with my lieutenant taking one archer with him. He is commander of the mission. If they can find and eliminate any small roving bands or

any slavers in pursuit of the boy they should eliminate them. They must be quiet and rely on stealth. It does no good to bring all of the slavers upon us in their greater numbers. They are to scout out the camp and return with news.

We reach the half time mark and I see Sean rise to relieve himself. He is sweating but he shoots me a grin anyway. I hope his scenario is not too impossible. I continue to write without a break.

Fourth: After the scouts' return and with the news of their success, we take the following action. I assume they were able to take out four to six of the enemy leaving the ratio basically one and a half to one. I leave one swordsman with the boy and the horses with orders to ride with the boy back to the main army if we do not return by morning.

Fifth: We stealthily surround the slavers camp at dusk. As night falls we begin to pick off their sentries by bow. We locate the trapped children and plan to attack from the opposite side to keep the danger as far away from the children as we can. I send my lieutenant and one archer around to where the children are being held. They should be able to dispatch any guards left around them after the assault begins on the other side of the camp.

Sixth: The assault: We stay in a tight group and enter the camp attacking any that try to stand against us. The archers cover our backs from the tree line and we make

quick work of the unsuspecting slavers. None are left alive.

Seventh: The children are released and we escort them to the nearest town where they can be collected by their parents. Minimal casualties expected.

"Time!" yelled the old knight. I let out a deep breath and take a look at my mates. Sean still has a grin on his face. He winks at me. The old knight takes up our parchment and joins a group of two other knights at his table. They read over each set of our strategies and talk in hushed voices to themselves.

I stand and stretch as Sean and Edward walk over to me. One of the other boys looks a little pale, and suddenly pukes. "Alright, Banion?" Sean asks. "Not too bad I guess. They had me leading a group of sixteen. Gave 'em the old stealth and assault," I told him.

"That's a big group!" Sean exclaimed. "I had only four with me, attacked at a pub we were. Right in the middle of dinner. Interesting that the strategy was not based solely on field warfare. Course, you know I don't like to be interrupted in my suppers."

We three laughed until we saw the old knight come back towards the table. He addressed the group: "Boys. Three of you have proven that you can think out a plan given the time. Remember, that this will not always be the case. The other two, I'm sorry to say, do not have the markings of a thinker that must be present in a knight of

Cork."

"Banion, and Sean…"

"Oh no! We didn't make it," I thought. All the shame. I couldn't make it through the first test."

"…and Edward. You have proven yourselves worthy. You may continue through the gate behind me and on towards the second test."

Sean embraced me, "Banion! We made it through! Luckily, me bashing in heads left and right is a good strategy. Sorry about the other two though. We looked and saw the other two boys led back the way we came. The puking boy and one that had begun to cry. They needed to keep their heads up. We would need them as soldiers if what my father said was true.

We clasped hands with Edward as he joined us from the table. He too was relieved and told us of his strategy at being alone and chased by a group of bandits. Luckily, he was able to use the terrain of the countryside against them.

CHAPTER 5

The skittish knight who had led us to the first trial showed back up at the gate and led us through. I heard whispers above us as we walked through a path lined by hedges. All of the sudden, I heard the most mysterious moan coming from an unseen distance off to our left. The knight half drew his sword before noticing our surprise and sheathing it hastily. This man was frightened of something that much was true. Maybe he had been in one too many battles and thought every noise at attack. It was probably one of the younger knights playing a trick on us. We reached a clearing where three paths met. Set before us was a veritable feast.

"Eat and regain your strength for the trials ahead," the skittish knight said to us. He then walked to the other side of the clearing and looked off into the trees as if searching for something. Sean began to tear ravenously into the meat and bread on the table. He would eat a whole horse if someone didn't tell him he could no longer ride it if he did. I nibbled on some cheese and bread as we waited for God knows what. This too could be part of the test.

A few minutes later from the other two paths came a knight leading the boys that had made it through the first tests of the other groups. One group still had four boys, and the other had three like ours. We were down to ten. One third of our mates had not made it through the first trial.

Were they always this tough? The old knight came up the path and informed us that we would have a half of an hour to rest and to eat. Each boy would then be taken, alone, and be tested for feats of arms. Any who made it past the second stage would meet up again together for the final test.

He then pointed at me and said, "Banion, your group has been here the longest, so you will come with me now. Sean, you will leave with Sir Gregory, and Edward you will leave with Sir Ivan."

We got up, shook hands with each other and began to head towards our leader. The old knight said nothing as he walked me down a path that I had not seen off to the side of the clearing. We walked for what seemed like an hour but it was probably much less.

Finally, up ahead of me I saw two knights dressed in full plate armor that were solid black without any devices standing near a stream. There was a fire in the clearing that had burned low. I couldn't make out who the two knights were because they had their visors down, and I had never seen this armor before.

The old knight turned to me and said, "You are riding through the woods and are stopped by these two knights blocking the road. React."

One of the two knights stepped towards me and said,

"You. You have insulted our family name by disgracing our sister. We will now kill you and let your blood pay for your transgression."

KILL ME? What was this? How is them trying to kill me part of the test. I also had only light padded armor on and these men had on full plate. I stood no chance against the two of them.

I replied "I did no such thing. My purity is my armor and I would never disrespect your family or your sister's name. You have the wrong man."

"You are Banion?" the other knight spat.

"Yes, but…" I looked around for the trial master, but he had disappeared. This seemed all wrong.

"No buts," The first knight said. "We know who you are, and we will have our vengeance."

At this the two knights drew their weapons. One had a battle axe that would cleave me right in two, and the other had a sword. I drew Oíche and readied myself not knowing if I was about to die or not.

Just then the words of Sir Jahnis came back to me. Think before you act. Assess the situation and do not rush in out of pride. Strategy. That was what I needed. I had nothing going for me in this fight. I'm sure they individually outmatched me with their weapons and they had armor.

What advantages did I have? I had speed and agility on my side. They would move slowly and with calculated steps. I could not let them corner me or it would be over. I needed to separate the two of them. I also had my wits. They expected me to run straight at them. So, I should give them what they wanted but with a slight deviation.

I ran towards the two knights that had crossed half the distance between us. I slid to a knee and kicked the ashes of the fire straight into the first knight's face. He coughed and gagged and swung his axe directly at my head. The good thing for me was that my head was no longer there.

As he rushed to uncover his face, I ran to his left, away from his brother. This put him in between us as an obstacle. I slashed down with Oíche into the back of his knee and pushed with all my strength. He tumbled over into the fire and scrambled to get up. It sure was a good thing for me that plate armor is heavy.

At this point the other knight had turned to face me and I parried his sword thrust with mine. I countered and began to slash and swing as quickly as I could. I hit him in the sword arm as he prepared to swing at me and felt a satisfying crunch of his metal arm piece. I paid for my victory with a solid punch in the face with a gauntleted hand that felt as if he had cracked my jaw. I stumbled away dazed and backpedaled away from him.

He roared in anger and came lumbering after me. I deftly jumped backwards over the stream just as the second knight charged and was upon me. He sank knee deep into the mud in the water, the plate weighing him down. I slapped away his feeble sword thrust with his weak arm and put Oíche to his throat.

"I yield, Master Banion." The knight said. I looked up and saw two of my father's knights rolling the other brother knight out of the fire. He was coughing and cursing, but seemed to be okay. I took my sword from the knight's throat and two more knights appeared out of nowhere to help him out of the mud. The old knight was suddenly at my side with a smirk on his face.

"You did quite well, Banion, considering you had two fully armored knights against you. I was glad to see you use strategy and your surroundings to your advantage. We do not fight only with our swords, but we fight with our minds and our wits. Your father will be proud to hear what you accomplished. Now onto another test. This one is a test of survival."

Chapter 6

The old knight handed me a longbow and a quiver of five arrows. He spoke, "A knight must often travel the roads in search of injustice in the king's name. When he does such he might be out of a town or castle for weeks at a time. He must be able to provide for himself in such times, and also for those that follow him. You have three hours of daylight left. You are to go on a hunt, kill suitable meal for three knights including yourself, and be back to the clearing where you ate your lunch by the time the moon is at its peak tonight. This is your test. Go."

A hunt? A test of my ability to be a knight is to see if I can go shoot a few hare or a deer in the woods? I have been doing this since I was old enough to hold a bow. But no, I should not question what they ask me to do. I didn't have time.

I ran into the woods as quickly as I could, following the stream. There was no time to spare. In very little time I found a game trail leading to the stream and followed it away from the water. I wondered to myself why I was really out here right now. The game masters could not have doubted that I could provide food for myself and others if need be.

I was blessed. I had had little difficulty in the two trials

I had faced during the day although I had been scared to death back by the stream. I just didn't know it until it was over. I wonder how fared Sean and Edward and if they also had a fight in the woods too and were then sent to fetch supper for our fathers? I have no doubt that Sean clobbered any opponent they put him up against. Even the older knights were giving him a wide berth after his most recent growth spurt.

I almost ran over the deer as I had my mind on other things. Luckily for me I had my arrow in hand with my bow or it would have gotten away. I shot quickly but the arrow flew true. Right in the doe's heart. It did not even register that I had rushed into the clearing before it knew nothing. I took a rope from my pack and strung up the deer and began to clean and dress it. Dark was upon me, but I knew that I would wear myself out if I tried to carry the deer back with all its entrails on the inside. I did not want to be tired when I faced the final trial. It could be immediate upon my return or they could wait until morning. I did not know. It took me close to an hour to clean the deer and prepare to return to the camp. I was not in possession of much time so I had to jog most of the way back but at an easy pace.

CHAPTER 7

As I crossed back over the stream and headed the last few miles back to camp, the weariness of the day started to come upon me. It had been close to fifteen hours since I left the castle and the moon was rising quickly overhead. The trials had taken their toll on my mind and my body and I was close to exhausted.

The weight of the dressed deer on my back seemed to grow with every step that I took. I kept expecting to hear laughter or see fire through the trees to mark my return to the trial-grounds. I looked up in the sky and checked the constellations to make sure that I was on the right path back to my friends and my father.

The moon was ever reaching higher into the sky. I felt like my time must be running out when finally I heard voices ahead. I broke through the last tangle of branches and burst into a clearing. There a great fire was burning and the fire was surrounded by the knights and some of the boys. I near collapsed next to the fire and dropped the deer onto the ground. The game maker walked over to me and said, "Well done Banion, not much time left, we were beginning to wonder if you would make it back at all."

A knight came forward and picked up my deer and began to prepare it for the flames. As he did so I felt a firm grasp on my shoulder and looked back to see a tired Sean, all smiles.

"A deer, Banion! I found not but some roots and berries and no game at all!"

Sean handed me a skin of water and I accepted graciously as I sat down next to my friend. The air was cooling off at a rapid pace and I was grateful for the fire at hand. I did not see mine or Sean's father in the clearing and the question must have been clear on my face.

"Our fathers are not here, Banion. Just the game makers and a few knights on watch."

I saw three boys asleep on the ground near us napping even before the food was ready.

"Nobody brought much food back." He pointed at Edward who came to join us from the other side of the fire. "Edward got a brace of rabbits with that sling shot o'his." Edward smiled as he joined us. "Only six of us left" said Edward. "I guess the other four did not pass through the test of arms trial. Either that or they got lost in the woods looking for food." We laughed at the thought but a sense of uneasiness followed it. The truth was: We were down to six after one day.

As we regrouped, the food was ready and we tore into it greedily. The roots, berries, and rabbit were put into a thick stew, and the deer we ate straight off the spit with our knives. As we ate, we shared with each other the stories of our test of arms. Sean had faced four men and had beaten them back with his great new hammer and unrelenting battle lust. Edward had faced two like me, and had broken one of their swords with his axe. He had almost gotten his arm chopped off as a result, but was able to foil that attack by bashing his assailant in the face with the handle of his axe at the last second.

As we talked the game master game up to our group and said, "Best get some rest boys. The final trial is mere hours away. You've come so far, you need to be vigilant tomorrow and prepared for anything." At that he walked over to the other group of boys where I assume he said the same thing. The knights on watch had begun to drift away and we were left alone.

"We should post our own watch tonight," I said. Sean replied, "I'll take the first, I have been back the longest and have been sitting on my arse!" "Great," I said, "I will follow, and then Edward will take us to dawn. Wake the next when you cannot keep your eyes open any longer." Agreed, I rolled over and fell asleep.

CHAPTER 8

I woke with a start hours later. The sky was graying in
the east. Dawn was approaching. I tried to roll over and fall
back asleep, but something just didn't feel right. As I sat up,
to my left, Sean tensed too and propped himself up as he
turned to me. "You feel it too?" He asked. I nodded and
saw Edward materialize out of the shadows across the
clearing. He whispered, "I'm glad you two are awake. I
cannot shake a funny feeling. It is quiet, too quiet. It was as
if the woods were trying to tell us something. It wants us to
pay attention.

I motioned for my friends to arm themselves and follow
me. Sean picked up his hammer, and Edward his axe and
shield. Thus armed we left our bedrolls and melted into the
tree line. We were tense, but we knew the woods well
enough to read its signs. There was a predator nearby and
we should not be caught off guard. I knew that Sean and
Edward were thinking the same as I. We thought the final
trial was probably a small pack of wolves or maybe even a
bear sent to test our alertness. Whatever the game master
could come up with to test us could be sent our way.

We retreated but kept the clearing in sight. The low
burning coals of the night's fire still glowed faintly and the
smell of smoke still hung over the air. That might scare
away most animals of the woods, but not the bigger

predators. Edward grabbed my arm and pointed three fingers towards the clearing and then at the ground. We had left the other three boys sleeping. A mistake, but one that we could not remedy now without blowing our cover and our safety.

A low rustling sound came from the woods on the other side of the clearing. The wind had picked up, but a breaking branch told us that it was more than the wind that was causing the noise. It did not come again for a few seconds. An odd smell came on the breeze. It was bitter, but sweet. A low moan broke the silence in the camp. One of the sleeping boys awoke. I was relieved. He stood and kicked his mate next to him. He drew a sword as he stood and faced the direction of the moan. Another one answered the first coming from twenty yards to the right of the first sound.

"Our fathers must be playing a prank on us," the first boy shouted. I grimaced as his voice rang out. He was stupid for giving away his position and letting whatever was coming know that he was awake. That had been his only advantage. His friend nodded and it was too late to warn them into silence. His friend yelled, "You don't scare us, knights!"

At this the moans sounded again. There were more this time, and they were closer. Sean leaned over to me. "They are going to get themselves killed. The fools." I nodded and pointed him to the left. He grinned as I turned to Edward. He nodded without direction and slipped into the shadows to my right. I saw him pull his sling out as he disappeared. I hated to use the other boys as bait, but whatever was coming was not giving us a choice.

I notched an arrow to my bow. From this distance, in the shadows, we would do better to let it play out and help where we could. The third boy had, by this time, added fuel to the fire and it flickered happily at the chance of life. The world was gray and growing brighter. Dawn was still half an hour away at best. At least the boy had the intelligence to kindle the fire.

The rustling leaves picked up again. At this point it became a shuffling. There was something coming. Of that much, I was sure. Multiple somethings if I was right. A moan once again pierced the silence. This one was close but the shadows on the far side of the camp were too much. On the edge of the clearing, ten yards from the boys in camp, a stooping figure shambled out. Its skin was as gray as the dawn. Its hair lank and matted. Its fingernails long, broken, and unkempt. I would have thought it a beggar from beyond the castle walls, but its eyes gave it away. They were dead and staring. The creature did not blink and its mouth hung open as if it could not keep it closed.

The boy with his sword drawn laughed heartily. "Our dads send us a starving bum as the final test! Back off, you!" He reached forward to push the creature back, not sensing the danger that was so apparent to me. His friends laughed as he did so. As his hand made contact, the creature's mouth shifted into a snarl and it lunged forward grabbing the boy's arm as it came.

The boy's laughed turned quickly into screams of pain

and rage as the monster took a bite out of his forearm. His friend stepped up quickly and pushed the creature back. It howled. It lunged forward again and the bleeding boy stepped up and thrust his sword into the creature's stomach with a yell of triumph. The sword buried itself deep. The creature continued forward, impaling itself as it came. It grabbed the boy's head and violently bashed at him with both hands.

Lost in his victory, the boy was unprepared for this counter attack. He fell under the beast and flailed wildly. His friends stepped in to help, and we waited. They threw the monster off and dragged their friend away. The creature was still thrashing around on the ground and then it slowly raised itself up. As the two boys turned back to the creature, from the camp's edge came five more of the creatures. Two pounced upon the boy on the ground and began biting him and beating him with their fists. I stood shocked. I watched as one of the boys cut off one creature's head as his shield mate gave one a mighty bash on the chest with a short hammer. Still the creatures came on relentless and determined.

It was time to act. I whistled once as I loosed my first arrow. I saw it strike one beast in the throat. My second arrow was away almost immediately when I saw a stone fly from my right crushing a monster in the head. It crumpled to the ground. One of the two remaining boys was down beneath another of the monsters. The one with my arrow in its neck joined in. The creature with the sword protruding from its chest harried the other boy and was pressing him back. At this I whistled twice. Two short bursts. I dropped my bow and quickly drew Oíche. As I stepped into the clearing Sean with his great hammer stepped out ten yards to my left and Edward with his axe and shield ten yards to my right.

It seemed that all this had happened in the matter of thirty seconds. Only one creature was down and the creatures immediately knew we were there. In synch, the three of us yelled out our war cries "Cork, Cork!" "Eire!" "Ireland!" We rushed in. To my left, I saw Sean deliver a gigantic blow crushing the spine of one of the two feeding monsters. Edward stepped up and slammed his shield into the creature attacking the boy. He fell back, relieved for the reinforcements. Two of the beasts ran towards me. It one quick motion I decapitated one of the beasts and cut the arm off the second. I kicked out and knocked the second sprawling.

I heard Sean yell and then heard a sickening thud as his next blow fell. If there was one thing about my friend that I never wanted to face, it was that new hammer in his hands. Before me, the one armed creature stood once again. Like in the earlier test in the clearing, time slowed down. My mind captured the entire scene instantly. These beasts did not fear pain. They looked human, but something was very wrong. It was as if our blows did not stun them at all. Three of them had fallen. One to a stone in the skull, one to a mighty blow that must have broken its spine, and the third to decapitation. The others were not fazed in the slightest by their mortal wounds. Of the three remaining, one had an arrow in the neck, the other a sword in the chest, and the third had an arm off.

I felt the odds were tipping in our favor. It was down to four versus three, but I felt victory too soon. Two more of the beasts came stumbling into the clearing at this point. "DESTROY THEIR HEADS!" I yelled, "IT'S THE ONLY WAY TO BRING THEM DOWN." At this the remaining boy ran forward with a mighty screech. Revenge was on his face and he rushed in blindly. He hit one of the two new creatures in the neck and his blade buried itself in the creature's collarbone. The second immediately closed in, biting the boy on the shoulder.

To my right, Edward rushed forward knocking one beast aside in an effort to save the boy. He hurled his axe through the air at it lodged in the bitey creature's head. The boy pulled out a dagger and stabbed the other through the eye and then collapsed as the two new creatures fell beside him. At this point, the one armed creature again rushed me. I held out the point of Oíche and, bracing myself, allowed the creature to run itself through. Oíche entered its mouth and its brains burst out the back of its head. I shook the creature off and saw Sean bash in the other creature's head, ending its feeding. One creature remained and Edward returned to it. The creature that had started it all stood against him with a sword protruding from its chest. Edward was weaponless, but I waited and watched to see what my friend would do.

Edward yelled as the beast ran towards him. He threw his shield at its legs and it tripped as it came towards him. Edward stepped to the side as the creature ran past him; he reached out and, pulling the sword from its chest, promptly and with finality lopped off its head. We were covered in gore as we stepped forward to regroup. The boy, to our side, wept as Edward retrieved his axe from the fallen creature and came back towards us.

"All well?" I asked. "Aye," Said Sean and Edward together. We looked at the creature on the ground before us. "What are they?" Edward asked. "Like men, but no more." Sean replied. "This must be the plague that the rumors have spoken of," I exclaimed. "There is no other explanation."

We realized the quiet almost too late. The weeping had stopped. We turned and saw that the boy ceased to live. We crossed ourselves, mumbling prayers for his soul. As we prayed, the most unnatural thing happened. The boy, who had been dead minutes before, turned. He opened his eyes and they were bloodshot, and as dark as night. "It has spread," Edward said. A moan escaped its lips and at that sound a crossbow bolt silenced it forever and woke us from our shock.

The anxious knight from before stepped out of the trees on the other side of the clearing; He was anxious no longer. He stooped and tore out the bolt from the boy's head and then went from body to body of the other boys driving a short blade into their skulls.

He looked up at us. "The bite spreads the infection." He said. "There is never much time after it happens before they turn." As he spoke, the woods behind him were filled with the sounds of men. Our fathers walked into the clearing.

Three knights rushed to their son's bodies and began to weep. Sean, Edward, and my fathers stepped forward along with the game master.

My father spoke, "Boys. Men. It does me good to see you standing." Before he came to us, the anxious knight had come forward with his ancient crossbow trained upon us. "Have you been bitten?" He asked. He circled us as we replied that we had not. It must have been hard to tell with the blood covering our bodies, but satisfied, he nodded and our fathers came forward and embraced us.

As my father stepped forward, I felt a huge weight lifted off my shoulders. It must have been the battle rage leaving my body, but I breathed for what I felt was the first time in ages. The smell of death hung heavily over the clearing.

The game master came toward the three of us and our fathers stepped back. "The final trial is over. You have faced what is the most apparent danger to the kingdom of Ireland in its history and you have lived. You three boys. Sean, Edward, and Banion, as game master, I pronounce the three of you knights."

My father stepped forward. "Kneel." We did as we were bade. He drew his sword, tapping the blade once on each of our shoulders. "As king of the southern kingdom, I recognize the three of you as knights of my court. Do you swear to uphold justice, fight for those that are in need, and protect our people from all that come against them?" We three answered together, "Aye."

"Good, I welcome you." My father said. "You have become men when Ireland needs you most. You must now travel to Dublin and get the high king's blessing as knights of the realm. You know the new danger that stalks our land. It will be our undoing, unless we can stop it. It spreads faster than we could imagine. Your journey will be long, and you will face many dangers, but the knights standing beside you are your only hope. We prepare for siege, you, Banion, must seek also the help of your uncle and spread this news as you travel."

Sir Jahnis stepped forward and said, "I welcome you brothers. Back to the castle. You have the night to rest, tell your family goodbye, and kiss your sweethearts. Tomorrow morning you ride north."

CHAPTER 9

It seemed almost like a dream as I rode back through the forest and back up the winding path to the castle. My father rode beside me and had a huge grin on his face but I could not engage him in conversation.

"I knew you'd make it, me boy! Never doubted ya for a second. I did wonder for a moment if you boys, ahem, men would notice the second attack of the creatures. Damn surprise wasn't it? We don't know much what to think at the moment, but to see how you three handled 'em, and used your heads too, it was just perfect…"

I let him continue with his boasting of us. I sat silent and tried to wrap my head around all that had happened in the last day. In reality, I wasn't proud at all. I feel like ever since I could hold a sword I had been training for this moment, but my anticipation and expectations were destroyed with the memory of those creatures biting and hitting the boy on the ground. And the one that continued on with a sword thrust through his middle.

I looked back and saw Sean and Edward with similar contemplative looks on their faces. Eventually our fathers must have noticed our mood, and chalking it up to exhaustion, fell silent beside us knowing that we would come around after having time to process.

Riding into the courtyard was difficult. The expectant looks on the faces of the entire court turned into a blur as mothers screamed and began to weep when their sons came back draped across the back of their horses instead of in the saddle themselves. I saw Edward's mother and little sister rush to his horse as he rode in behind me. Tears for a totally different reason. Sean and my father already knew our success so they gruffly dismounted and handed their reins to awaiting attendants. We stood behind them as my father turned to address the court at the top of the stairs. All sound stopped as he began to speak.

"Ladies and gentlemen of the court, it is with sadness that I see the grief so plain on mothers' faces. We had fifteen boys of age when we left yesterday. In a time of uncertainty, we hold the trials as in ancient custom. Seven of those boys were deemed not fit to lead as knights of the realm. There is no dishonor in this, but only a different path that God has placed before them. These boys will become master soldiers and one day perhaps, lead men of their own in our lord's army. Two boys were injured during the test of arms trial, and upon recovery will serve in my household. No man injured in the service of Cork will be left without food in their bellies while I am king."

There were cheers at the graciousness of the king. Everyone knows that if you are injured in such a way that you cannot fight or farm then there is not much use for you but charity in this cruel world. My father always found some way to employ his veterans though. The king continued:

"I grieve with the mothers and fathers of three. Three of our boys lost their lives in the final trial. Their memories are to be forever immortalized on the weeping stone alongside their ancestors and their ancestors' ancestors. We lift up their souls to the father of heaven and ask for his mercy upon them.

Lastly, it is with great honor and pride that I congratulate three men of Cork who have become knights of Éire this morn. Banion, my son, prince of Cork, (cheers erupted at this proclamation), Sean Ó'Sullivan (more cheers), and Edward Conleigh."

The crowd applauded in the midst of the grief and lamentations of sonless mothers. It made me slightly sick, but I knew my duty and stood stoically by. The king dismissed us to rest and began giving orders for burials to be arranged and wakes to be planned. Being the king's son, I had to shake hands with many knights and courtiers on my way to my chambers. Somehow they all managed to be in my way so that I could not escape.

I saw Sean head up the stairs and he gave me a salute as he escaped. He then pressed four of his fingers horizontally towards his open palm and then with the same hand he pointed one towards the ground. It seemed to me that our childhood was ancient history after what I had seen the previous day, but I couldn't help but smile as I understood Sean's message. Four o'clock, after we sleep. I caught Edward's eye and he nodded showing that he too had seen Sean's message. We would rest, and then we would plan.

CHAPTER 10

Fang knocked me over as I opened my chamber door.
He licked my face and yipped in my ear. He then proceeded
to sit on my chest and I could not control myself any
longer. I burst into laughter at his excitement and then
moaned as I realized the five stone dog did not intend to get
off any time soon. After punching him in the side a few
times he got off, wagging his tail, and I followed him into
the room. I felt as if I could breathe for the first time all
day. I shuttered the windows and collapsed into my bed
without fully undressing. Fang immediately jumped up
beside me and turned towards the door before settling in.
He was the best watch dog one could ever have.

I woke with a start some hours later sore but feeling
much more alert and refreshed. There was a tray with some
food on it sitting on the table which surprised me knowing
that Fang was in the room. I discovered him on the floor by
the foot of my bed gnawing on a rather large bone. That
would explain how my food was untouched. I crossed over
to the window and threw back the curtains, checking the
sun's position as it stung my eyes. Early afternoon by my
guess. I would soon go meet Edward and Sean.

A maidservant entered from the other room telling me
that she had heated water for a bath. I realized she must
have been what woke me up, and thanked her as I headed

in. The bath was perfect. I washed the grime off and spent a few minutes just soaking. I thought of the fact that I was now Sir Banion and a smile touched my lips. The undying creatures seemed a world and an age away so I put them out of mind.

I dressed myself in a moss green tunic and leather breeches knowing that there would be a feast that night in our honor. I strapped Oíche to my waist because I would now be expected to always be armed as a knight of the realm. It felt natural to have the weight on my left hip and I felt confident as I pulled my boots on and headed to the tower to meet my friends.

We talked for an hour about all that had happened. We addressed each other as Sir Banion, Edward, and Sean as much as we could out of fun and to get used to hearing it said out loud. My friends were also a little shaken up about the final trial, but we knew we were not expected to face it alone.

"The really did crumple quite easily once we figured out a thing or two about 'em" Sean said.
    "Yes," Edward answered "but that was only a handful of them and to be fair they were distracted by far easier prey."
    I thought aloud, "how many do you think there are?"
"Loads and loads of them if I'm thinking correctly" replied Sean.

"Sean, you know what happens when you spend a lot of time thinking!"

We all laughed at Edward's joke and then settled as we grasped the reality and truth of Sean's words. Whatever it was, this plague, it spread quickly and without much effort. There really could be "loads and loads of them" out there waiting for us.

We all stood knowing that we would be expected in the great hall soon. My friends paused as I drew my blade and held it before me. "Together or not at all lads." We three repeated the vow together, with weapons crossed, and knew we did not stand alone.

The feast was much as we expected. There was much merriment, drinking, and sport. Sir Gareth even came over and congratulated me on my knighthood. He told me that they would all need someone like me soon enough. I did not know what he meant, but was quickly distracted by an outrageous belch coming from Sean's direction. I saw the anxious knight with the crossbow from the trials sitting at my father's side and whispering together with him as they ate. Sir Jahnis sat with them as well as Edward and Sean's fathers. They seemed to be having a good time and all the men were bent on every word the anxious knight said. He must have joked because they all exploded in laughter at the same time.

I turned back to my friends as we were all wished well by a passing drunken man-at-arms. "Keep yer shords in yer scabbberds me boys if ye stay long in Dublin. No telling what kind er trouble ye can get em in!" He stumbled away laughing as he was hailed by some other knights across the room. He fell flat on his face as he ran towards them and came up with a busted tankard in his hand and a confused look on his face. The hall burst into laughter and added a call for the refilling of cups. Much later in the evening the mirth was slowed by my father standing to his feet and calling for quiet.

"Ladies and gentlemen of my court, we honor these three young men who have risen to the rank of knighthood this day. Slainté!

As we call this feast to a close we remember all that have fallen in service to our kingdom. We honor their memories! Slainté! I now call these three new knights forward."

We rose and faced him.

"Boys, you know that you must travel to Dublin and seek the high king's favor. We have sent a message ahead of you and the high king expects you. I'm afraid that Éire is not the same country she was just a few days ago, so I do not know what you will face on the road, but I do know the road is different than it was. You three shall not travel alone, but in the company of one more. Sir Walter Saxon our friend from across the sea shall travel with you and see you safely for part of the way before he continues on his own errands."

The anxious knight stood and went to my father's side as he said this. So he was English. That explains a lot. My father continued:

"Your errand will not be easy. Cork will need help in the coming months that only the high king can provide. So you will have to secure these from your uncle, Banion, as well as getting his blessing. We prepare for a new enemy here at home. You leave at first light, lads. Best to bed." The hall stood and yelled praise for us. Sir Jahnis winked at me as I headed out of the hall. I went to sleep heavy headed as I wondered what would happen next.

CHAPTER 11

I awoke well before first light and started putting
together my pack. Father had been in to see me already and
told me that he wanted us to take the longer route through
the countryside rather than taking the king's highway. The
journey would take us less than a fortnight if the weather
permitted and we could make good time. This was Ireland
though so I didn't have any high hopes for a sunny and
warm trip.

As I put together my pack I thought of all I would need.
A good knight carries only what is necessary. This included
arms and armor, and food. I knew my father would have
the food prepared for all of us so I gathered an extra shirt
and several pairs of thick wool socks. A good soldier
knows that if he doesn't take care of his feet, his feet won't
take care of him, and a knight that cannot walk, cannot
fight.

I strapped on Oíche and made sure the leather strap was
strong. I tied two extras around the sheathe in case I needed
replacements. Before putting my boots on, I wrapped an
extra bow cord around each of my lower calves so that they
would be kept dry even in the rain. A bow was useless
without a dry cord. I wrapped another around my right
bicep so that my leather shirt would cover it. This would be
the easy one to get to in a hurry if need be. On my right hip

I hung a Seax. This short, broad blade was thick enough to parry a sword with in a bind, although I wouldn't want to have to do it twice. A hunting knife I tucked into my left boot. This was all I would carry on my person. I was never much for shields even though I have one because I preferred not to have my balance encumbered by its weight. I lost my speed advantage in this case.

I called to Fang as I looked back at my room before leaving. For some reason, I felt like I was saying goodbye to the chambers of my childhood and walking out the door in search of my adult life. Fang raced me down the stairs and into the great hall. I ate a hurried breakfast and headed out to the stables to check on my horse. There I met Sean and Edward and we all double checked our own strappings and then each other's. When we were all satisfied that our horses were in good condition, we walked them out to the front of the castle.

The sun was coming up as we were met by my father as he came out of the front of the castle. With him was Sir Walter, the English guide, and Sean and Edward's fathers. My father snapped his fingers and servants came out bearing sacks of food and provisions for each of us. We added them to our packs and prepared to say farewell.

Sir Walter interrupted by climbing on his own horse that stood by already pointing toward the gates. My father came forward and grasped my arm and pulled me close.

"You are me only boy. I love ye son. You take care of yourself and the lads, and listen to Walter. He has more experience with these things than anyone and you can trust him. Don't be careless, me boy."

With that we parted. Sean and Edward reined in next to me and we all looked back at our fathers. They held up their hands as we followed Sir Walter down the street and out the castle gates. We were on our way.

CHAPTER 12

It didn't take long to be in the middle of nowhere. The
next few days were a blur of greenery and saddle soreness.
We made good time, but were two weeks out from Dublin
if we didn't slow our pace at all. We were in good spirits.
For us, this was heaven. We were traveling the open road
with our best friends and had the freedom none of us had
really experienced having grown up in the castle with
duties and training.

It was about noon when we stopped for a break. Sean
tripped getting out of the saddle and almost knocked
himself out on a fallen tree. Edward and I screeched in
laughter. We were cut short upon seeing Sir Walter go stiff
next to his horse.

"Quiet boys!" He hushed us quickly. We stood waiting,
watching for his cue. At his signal, we tied the horses to the
tree as he slipped off into the brush. The three of us drew
blade and fanned out and watched the perimeter of the
camp. Suddenly, Walter was back amongst us.

"There are a group of men up the road. I would bet
they are bandits judging by their camp. They are off to the
side waiting in ambush for any who are unlucky enough to
pass by. They total seven." Edward looked to me and asked
what our next steps were. I looked over to Sean and saw the

beginnings of a grin stretch across his face. "We remove this menace." I said confidently. We were well trained and well armed. As knights of Cork, we were charged with the safety of the king's roads. This was our time. As our first official act as knights, we would end this terror.

I looked to Walter. "Any sentries, Sir?" Walter shook his head and laughed. "They've no idea we are here. It'll be like stealing biscuits from a baby.

"Stealth, lads." I said. "I pointed to Edward's sling shot. "Sir Walter and I will use our bows and take out at least one apiece. Edward, get another. That puts us even. Walter and I will cover Sean as he attacks, and Edward you join him if you don't have a second shot. We might be able to get them to give up if we take a few down. "

We all agreed and split up. Walter and Edward went left, Sean went right up the middle towards them, and I headed to the right with Fang at my heels. This would allow us to surround them and have Sean covered from every angle.

The brigands were snoozing around a small fire off the road. They had laid out spikes in the road to trip up any horses, an ugly thing to do. Half the men were not paying attention at all as we snuck up on them. A couple were looking the other way up the road. This might be easy after all.

I let out a sharp whistle after taking aim at what must have been their leader. My second arrow was on the string before the first hit him straight in the middle of the chest.

I saw two men on either side of him drop at the same moment. One with Walter's feathered shaft in his throat, and another with a stone in the eye. I heard Sean bellow his war cry as he rushed right up the road at them. By the time they noticed we were there, three were dead, and I put an arrow into the ground between the rest that were snoozing on the ground. They were fools though. They either did not get my message at all, or they didn't care.

They roared as they rose to their feet and scrambled for weapons. Sean was on them in a heartbeat. He pushed two of them over with his massive hammer. He then swung out wide and brought his hammer down on the collarbone of one that got too close. There was a sickening crack, but he had moved on by the time the sound reached me. I had to pause and respect the brute strength of my best friend. He had crushed the legs of the other one standing and turned as another had regained his feet and ran towards him. He was caught in the ribs by another of Walter's arrows and thrown sideways several yards. The power of the longbow always amazes me.

The last man dropped to his knees before Sean rather than join his comrades in death. Fang pounced on him, rolling him over on his back and standing on his chest, teeth bared, inches away from his face. He immediately began to beg for his life. The rest of us entered the scene and his eyes went wide with fear. He was young. Not much older than Sean, Edward, and I.

"Sir Knights. I beg your pardon. Puh, puh, please spare me.

I've only been with these guys for a week."

I addressed him: " Laddie, how did you get mixed up with this lot?"

He answered: "I beg you, sir. I was just trying to earn some coin for my family. I lost my job in the village because the miller has gotten sick and he kicked me out. He was practically crazed about it. I don't know what was wrong with him."

This was not a good sign. I asked him which village he was from and how far away it was. It was about a day away, and they had come out here so that they could catch people where two crossing roads merged into this highway.

"Listen boy, you run back to your village. You tell them that the knights of Cork protect these roads and their village and we will not tolerate robbers. No matter how desperate their situations are."

He ran off and we retrieved our arrows and stacked the bodies. We would pay someone in the village to come back here and bury them. Maybe even this boy that we let run off. We would need to go investigate this village and hope that his tale was true.

Edward perked up as we congratulated each other and a successful first mission. "Everybody like how ole Banion went all puffy chested with the king's authority? Scared the living breath out of that lad. hahahaha!" We all had a good laugh and went back to gather the horses. So much for a break for lunch.

CHAPTER 13

We ate hurriedly while in the saddle as we made our way up the road towards the boy's village. As he left he told us that his village, Baile Láibe, was a day away by foot, and that we only needed to follow the road and it would take us straight there.

We didn't know what to expect in this village, so as we rode we began to ask Sir Walter for more information on what we would face. I asked him, "Sir Walter, what can you tell us about the plague itself? Where does it come from? What does it do?

He coughed a little in his throat as he continued the restless search of his eyes from right to left as he rode. This man knew to expect danger at any time. We would learn much from him.

"Well, Master Banion, I first encountered it on the mainland. It was a single boy in the village that had come down with a weird sickness. The local priests had even been called to exorcise him after all healing remedies failed. I was on a mission from the English king to investigate the rumors of a new plague traveling through France. Some local priests told me to come pray for the boy, hoping that a Christian knight who had fought in the Holy Land would be able to bless him into health. This would be enough cover for me to be in France in the first place.

I went to a small shack with the village priest by my side prepared to see a boy sick with some unknown ailment, but what we found was even worse. The boy had turned during the night and had killed his mother and sister. He was feeding on his sister in the doorway to the home as if he had caught her while she tried to escape.

When we arrived, he left her body and ran at the priest. I stepped in the way and checked him with my shield, drawing my sword. He savagely beat at my shield, and then he pulled it down and I saw over the top of the rim and looked directly into his dead and distant, black eyes. I knew then that he was not a creature of God, and I stabbed him through the heart. If only I did not learn the next lesson so late.

Engulfed in my grief after stabbing the boy, I knelt to pray for his soul. As I did, he rose from death and attacked the priest and bit him. I cut off his head just as his mother and sister rose from their deaths. I noticed that the boy did not rise again and gave to his family the same mercy that I had just discovered for him. When I turned back, the priest was gone. He had fled after he must have realized what had happened to him. I called the men of the village to help me search for him, but we could not find him.

We burned the bodies of the dead family, and I told the priests what had transpired. I left the following morning, pained and heartbroken and confused in search of the priest. It wasn't until that afternoon that I realized my mistake and road back to the village with great haste. There was blood everywhere, but no bodies. A quarter of the village had been burned down. All I could find was a blood stained rosary nailed on the door of the orphanage, and barefooted tracks leading in all directions. I then faced the entire village that had been turned into the creatures and killed many. It was the single hardest experience of my life. I then walked back to the coast with some in tow and brought the evidence of the plague across the channel with me.

I still carry the rosary with me to remind me of my mission to never leave this plague where I can find it. The plague hits every person differently. I have seen them turn within minutes of being bitten, and as with the case of the boy and the priest, it was not until the next day that they were burdened with its curse."

The three of us sat open mouthed at Sir Walter's story. He later told us that this first encounter had not even been a full month ago, and he had already heard of villages disappearing in England, Scotland, Wales, and Cornwall. That is why his king had sent him to my uncle in Dublin, to warn him of what was coming, and to prepare Ireland for the battle that would come. My uncle had charged him with bringing the news to my father in Cork, finding a way to reveal it in the trials, and then my father had asked him to continue with his message to the rest of Ireland. We had learned much, but I still feel like we had no idea of what we were going to have to deal with.

CHAPTER 14

We made camp as the sun faded away in the west. We
could not travel any further in the dark for fear of one of
the horses breaking a leg. The village we were looking for
was so small as well that we did not want to pass it in the
night. This would allow us to ride into the village early in
the morning as everyone was waking up and as the village
business was getting underway. We all had different shifts
on watch throughout the night and we could all agree that
the weirdest thing was that none of us saw or heard
anything. This was exceptionally unexpected as one would
expect to hear the hoot of an owl, or see the eyes of the
night creatures like a wolf as we watched, but there was
nothing. We all saddled our horses the next morning with
an impending feeling of dread as we got back on the road to
the village.

Sir Walter left us early to scout out the road ahead and
Fang ran off into the woods to hunt. We rode together in a
tense state of unknowing. Sean struggled to get us all into
conversation as was his way. "What do you think we will
find at the village, lads? Here's to hoping a nice mug o' ale
and a full Irish breakfast. This dried meat and the
occasional apple is just not working for me."

Edward replied with his usual snarkiness, "It has barely
been a week on the road, Sean, and you are already starving

to death? God knows you could go a few days without the full breakfast. Look at that stomach!"

With that Sean took a playful swing at Edward's face from his horse and almost fell off into the mud. We had forgotten the pressure we felt earlier in the morning and were laughing as we saw Sir Walter riding back down the road towards us.

As he reigned in beside us the smiles fell off of our faces and he began to speak. "Lads, I am worried the plague has gotten to the village before we have, Jesu be with them. I saw no evidence of townsfolk within the boundaries of the village fields. I searched to the east and west of the village and there were no people working and no smoke from cook fires in the houses. Ready yourselves. We might have a fight on our hands."

It took us another two hours to reach the boundaries of the village fields. We stopped and donned our armor. Each of us wore chainmail over a leather jerkin with simple cloth underclothes. On our heads the chainmail continued up but left our faces clear and free. We wore thick leather gloves with steel ringlets sewn across the backs, and we wore plate armor greaves on our legs to protect our lower legs. The rest of our armor we left with our two pack horses as well as the extra courser that we had in case one of our war horses was injured.

We did not don all of our armor for fear that it would slow us down too much if we got surrounded. We remounted our horses and loosened our swords in their scabbards. I nocked an arrow to my longbow and held it in my left hand as we rode. Sir Walter loaded his ancient crossbow before mounting and gave it to Sean before he strung his own longbow. That would give Sean one long range shot before he dismounted and charged in with his hammer. One shot could make a huge difference depending on what we faced.

Edward had his slingshot out, and his pouch of steel projectiles loosened on his belt. He was deadly accurate with that sling. We were taking no chances as we rode into the village. We would look rather silly if we were wrong and rode into the village center armed to the teeth, but it was better to be safe than sorry. Edward offered up a prayer to the almighty for our safety as we did the king and God's' work in this village, and we rode forward not knowing what to truly expect from the next steps on this quest of ours.

We rode in a diamond formation into the outer streets of the village. If a village is what you could actually call this place. It was really a mismatched clump of small and dirty stone buildings gathered in no particular pattern clustered around a single church steeple. There were no people anywhere to be found. No dirty faces peeking out from behind half closed shutters, and no small unwashed children following the knights on horses with their mouths hanging open in awe.

We made it to the village square before we saw anyone although we did notice the footprints all over the ground that had been relatively undisturbed by horses or carts. In the middle of the square sat the boy we had released the day before. He was on his knees with a woman in his arms and even at a distance we could see his shoulders racked with sobs. I pointed Sean to the left and Edward to the right remembering our final trial that seemed like it was ages ago and was only a week in the past. Sir Walter and I dismounted and walked slowly towards the boy with our bows still in our hands, nocked and ready to be used at the slightest need. We circled him to approach him from the front. You did not want to sneak up on anyone wrought with such emotion. You could not know how they would react.

"Boy." Sir Walter said after a few moments. "What has happened here?"

The boy froze at the sound of his voice and slowly raised his eyes. A faint gasp escaped him as if in relief.

"Sir Knights." He said, "You are too late. They are dead. All of them. Even me sweet ma."

He broke again into sobs and Sir Walter and I exchanged worried glances. We signaled for Sean and Edward to rejoin us and they did after tying their horses with ours.

We filled them in on what we had heard and we all looked over our shoulders on cue as if we could feel that we were being watched. It was at that moment that the boy screamed.

"Mother! You're alive. We turned as she grabbed him

and took a huge bite out of his neck. His mother had come back to life in his arms, and he did not know the danger, but we had. This made this our mistake. His screams changed from happiness to fear and pain in an instant. He was unable to remove her from him as she continued to bite him over and over. Edward's arm quickly rose and the steel marble was released in an instant. The boy's mother stopped moving as the boy cried in agony.

"Silence him quickly!" Sir Walter hissed, and Edward mercifully shot the boy as well. He would have been dead in minutes, but they would have been minutes of absolute torture and pain. As the boys cries died away, we heard a low moan carried on the wind from the north. We all turned, having been distracted by the attack and death of the boy and his mother.

A single man stood in the street across from where we had entered the village square. Another moan escaped his lips as his dead eyes searched for us. It was answered from the east. Moans carried to us from the direction we had come. It was in an instant that we heard their dead cries from all sides. It was as if they were summoning one another to feast. The boy's death screams had announced our presence and we stupidly had allowed ourselves to get surrounded. It seemed as if we had found the rest of the villagers, or rather the villagers had found us.

We were surrounded by plague ravaged villagers that two days before were living their lives as if all were completely ordinary. I thought back to my own life two days before. We were delivering the king's justice on the roads of Ireland and it was as if this plague was not even real. The trials had been over for over a week and the immediate threat of the third trial had disappeared. Now, dozens of villagers brought reality crashing back down around us.

Sir Walter began giving orders almost immediately. "Sean you will fire the crossbow, and then use that big hammer of yours to keep them off our fronts as we fire. We all fire everything we've got. Remember you must hit them in the head or you have wasted your shot. Edward to the west, Banion to the north, I'll watch the east. Keep them off from the south, Sean. Now!"

My second arrow was away by the time the echoes of his words had left the square. I heard the sharp twang of Walter's longbow singing alongside my own. I heard the metallic clink as Sean fired the crossbow, and heard him bellow a challenge of war as he brought his hammer around. I could hear the swift zip of Edward's steel marbles and the sharp snap as each of his shots found its mark. We shot all that we had. I had over a dozen arrows that all released a tortured villager from this plague.

The bodies began to pile into a small wall around us which tripped several creatures as they came at us. As they began to hear our noise of war and perhaps instinctively smell us as their prey, they began to stumble at greater speeds as if they didn't want us to go away. I drew Oíche and severed the head of the nearest creature as it approached me. Now that our projectiles had worn themselves out, we tightened our grouping. Backing into a small square so that we could watch each other's flank.

During a short respite, as my attackers made their way towards me and a shambling pace, I turned to check on my brothers and saw Edward bashing one creature in the head with his shield while simultaneously chopping another through the spine with his axe. He twirled and blocked the next creature as it came at him, knocking it off its feet then he brought the bottom rim of his shield down through its mouth.

Sean was grunting and screaming at every swing of his axe, and he seemed tireless in the wake of the unyielding attack from hell. He cursed as he faced the town blacksmith. A large man with dead eyes and pounds of muscle covering his body from his work at his fires. He caught Sean's first swing right on his shoulder and I saw the arm go limp at the blow, but this did not stop his attack on Sean. Sean's face showed surprise as the blow that would have killed an ox hardly slow his attacker.

He grasped his hammer with both hands and struck out into the blacksmith's chest which checked his step just enough for Sean to flip his hammer over in his hands and drive the spiked point into the side of the creature's head. Sean laughed at his victory and continued his work. I began to wonder if Fang would make a reappearance from his hunt, or if he had wandered too far.

The battle seemed to slow for a moment as we all made short work of these slow creatures. We killed many of the creatures but more continued to arrive as the sound of our fight called them from the outer parts of the village. Rage contorted Walter's face as he slew on both right and left hands covering himself in gore. The battle lust was upon him, and perhaps he remembered all the innocents he had ever seen taken by this plague and his strength came with his desire that no one else should suffer this fate. My arm began to tire and Oíche began to feel like lead in my hand. I switched hands and continued to deliver these poor people that we had not been in time to save. The fight seemed to last for ages, but as it ended, we noticed that the sun had hardly made any movement across its daily route in the sky. We guessed later that we had fought for an hour without respite.

Sean leaned wearily on his hammer as Edward dispatched the final creature in his path. "Whew, this is tiring work we have gotten ourselves into." He said with gusto. We looked at one another and realized the truth to his words. Sir Walter answered him, "Our work is just beginning for today and the rest of our lives. We must give these villagers the burials they deserve as God's children. Come, we will make a funeral pyre for them, and honor them as Ireland's first victims to this curse of the devil."

We spent hours gathering the dead, tearing down small buildings to light the fire, and erecting warnings for others to not enter the village for fear of death. We took small rest one at a time to stand watch on the roof of the town hall. The view there commanded a look in all directions and we could clearly see if anyone was approaching the town. A few creatures straggled in late as we worked, and the watchman, without fail, was able to dispatch them before they approached one of his fellows.

We all worked silently and did our duty to the people of this village. It was not proud work, but it was something that must be done. At once, on the far side of the square, Edward was lifting a body when a creature underneath grabbed him and bit his ankle. He screamed in fear as he tore a hatchet off of his belt to dispatch the beast. We all came running to his aid and found him sitting and cursing the poor creature that had gotten him. Walter quickly went to Edward's side and checked his ankle. Edward said, "Lads, it's over for me you will have to kill me so that I do not come back as one of these... things. I won't have it said that I let myself hurt my friends.

We were in shock at the prospect of one of us being bitten so soon on our mission. Walter laughed aloud in that moment and Sean gave him a look of utter anger. When Walter noticed he quickly shared that the creature's teeth had not bitten through Edward's boot. He had Edward remove his boot and we all checked. He had a bruise already beginning to appear, but his skin was not broken. Walter shared how that even though it had hurt like hell, Edward would not be leaving us so soon. Tears came to Edward's eyes as the realization came over him. We all grabbed on to him and even were able to laugh. We did not laugh out of humor, but just because our emotions did not know how to respond in any other way.

We fortified the town hall on the square that night and took shifts to sleep. Two of us stayed awake and tended the funeral pyre while the other two, in exhaustion, took their chance to recover. The following morning, Walter decided that we should stay another day in the village and recover from the ordeal of the last few days on the road from the bandits to the villagers. We all gladly agreed and spent the day recovering and discussing strategy for what we should do next.

CHAPTER 15

I woke before the sun started to rise in the east. Walter was on guard and he nodded to me as he noticed that I was awake and slipped off into the shadows. I had a mind to lie back down and get as much rest as I could but the weight of what we were facing made me restless. I pictured the poor boy from the morning before, holding his mother, the fear on his face, and the disbelief in his screams. I packed my saddle bags and then I pulled out Oíche and began to sharpen the blade. I stepped out into the street and checked my surroundings.

I saw Sir Walter pass between two of the buildings to the west as he continued his rounds. I heard a twig snap in the bushes not far from the town hall and drew Oíche as I made my way over to the side of the building. It would not surprise me that there were still a few villagers straggling in with the smells and noises of the burning we had done the previous day and night. I gripped my sword with casual easiness as I peered into the bushes, but the dawn was coming too slowly for me to be able to see yet.

The branches shivered and I took a step back and readied myself into a fighting stance. Suddenly, Fang sprang out of the bushes with a bloody maw and padded over to me with the casual swagger of a predator that fears little. I yelled and then laughed as his eyes rolled and his tongue hung languidly out of his mouth as he approached me. I knelt and gathered him into a hug as I felt like our group was finally whole again.

"You missed all the excitement, Fang!" I spoke as I rubbed his ears. He yipped at me and bit at my hand playfully as I petted him.

"Looks to me like his hunt must have been successful," Walter said as he approached after his last circuit of the perimeter. Sean and Edward came sleepily out of the building with their weapons drawn. They must have heard my shout of surprise as Fang showed up. Each, in turn, took a moment to welcome Fang back.

The wolf had a way of calming all of our nerves. He was a fierce and loyal companion to our group and had quickly accepted Walter as we set out days before. A sense of easiness came over us with the realization that Fang would know if any danger was close to us long before we did.

Sir Walter called us back from our momentary lapse into boyish frivolity with a stern word. "Lads, this plague is traveling way faster than it should be. I'm afraid that Ireland is facing this threat of the future now. The king and I have estimated that, if unchecked, the sickness would have covered England by the end of summer, and not be to Ireland until next winter. We do not know if the northern cold will affect the creatures or not.

What I do know now is that our estimates were way

wrong. In order for this plague to have a serious outbreak in Ireland before summer is even in full swing means that it is here now, and we have to do something to stop it. I have to warn the other holdfasts in the west. I cannot continue on with you lads any further north. I'll travel towards Galway today and spread the news as I go. Your mission stays the same. You must still go to Sir Banion's uncle in Dublin and seek his blessing and his aid for Cork, and you must destroy any creatures that you come across. Do not leave any behind. We cannot let them take over this island. It has been an honor fighting alongside you, and I consider you all to be friends." With that, Sir Walter packed up his things, put them on his pack horse, embraced us all and rode out of the village heading west.

CHAPTER 16

It was so sudden that Sir Walter left that we did not know what to do with ourselves. For the last two weeks, Sir Walter had been the experienced adult guide for our trip to Dublin. Now we were on our own. We would truly have to make our own decisions and lead our own quest now. We gathered around to make our decisions on where we would head to next. Fang patrolled the area as we spoke together and watched for any signs of the plague wracked creatures that have recently come to our shores.

I said, "Friends, losing Sir Walter has me worried. No other person in all of Europe knows more about what we face than him, and he was a considerable force to have by our side in a fight too!"

Sean looked a little confused as if he had not fully grasped the fact that Walter was gone yet and the implications of we three being alone on the trail. Edward was honing the blade on his axe with frightful determination. The fact was that the three of us had never been alone before. Sure, we had gone off into the woods to camp as we grew up, but we were also pretty sure that my father had men out there looking after us as well. Now, rather quickly, and still covered in the gore of our recent fight, we stood at a crossroads.

At the time, we did not notice that it was at this point that our fate was decided. We could have turned home, ridden back to Cork with the news that the plague was already on our fair land and that we should prepare for defense. Then we would have just been my father's knights helping to battle the foes of Cork, but there was more at stake than Cork.

All of Ireland was under attack and Cork had high stone walls. The people in the country were under our protection too, and it was our duty to protect them as well as we could even if it meant giving up our own lives to do it. Plus, my father had given us a mission. We had to continue on our way to Dublin because our duty was to our liege lord and he had called on us to gather aid for the defense of our home. We could not fail in this mission.

I looked at my friends and gathered all the courage I could within my heart. "We must continue on. We have a duty to the people of Ireland and a mission to complete. Like Walter, we must spread the word and make our way north. I would rather not be here with anyone else than you two."

Edward glanced up at me and nodded his head. Sean stood and smiled. He laughed as he said, "They do go down pretty easy don't they!" And that was all it took. We laughed, took our belongings down to the stream and washed the gore off of our armor and weapons and dried them with some nearby hay. We spent the rest of the day cleaning up the battle. There would be no villagers coming back here and we could not risk the infection spreading.

We continued the large funeral pyre in the middle of the square and took turns with watch. Edward spent the afternoon fortifying the town hall so that we would be safe that night. We all retired there well after darkness had fallen, exhausted. We all quickly fell asleep as we knew that Fang would wake us if any danger appeared near the village. It had been an emotionally and physically draining day.

Fang woke us with a bark as dawn was creeping over the distant hills to the east. The three of us had slept through the night without bother. We owed Fang for this rest. I patted his head and gave him a big piece of dried meat from my pack. He carried it over into the corner to gnaw on it in peace and the rest of us checked the perimeter through the slits in the windows that Edward had left open.

There were two of the gray people in the town center as we went out, and Edward put them down quietly with his slingshot. Sean walked by grunting hello and went off around the side of the building to take care of his morning business. We packed up the horses after eating a rather boring breakfast and prepared to leave, but something just didn't feel right to me.

I felt that the village should be avoided at all costs, but nothing we did would keep out wanderers or traders coming through like usual. I gritted my teeth and got off my horse telling my companions my worry. I hated what I did next, but it had to be done. I went to the two gray people that Edward had killed earlier, drew Oíche and cut off both of their heads. Sean made two stakes for me as I did this, and we planted the stakes on the outskirts of the village where the king's road comes in from the north and from the southeast. This would be the way that most travelers came to the village, it was the way we had come after all, and this warning would be enough.

We also gathered two boards and crossed them underneath the heads so that there would be a large X there as a warning. The average Irishman was superstitious and this warning would do the work that we intended it to do. I looked at the dead gray head with the X below it and hoped that it would keep the unaware away.

Feeling as if we had done all we could do for this poor village, the first victims of Ireland's bane, we rode out on the king's road headed north. We did not know what lay ahead of us, but we knew that our gruesome task was only getting started.

Chapter 17

We rode for hours north on the King's road. The camaraderie of the road kept all of us in a good mood although we never were able to drop our guards. We had long stretches of not seeing any life but then we would have to rein in the horses as a herd of deer would flee across the path in front of us heading west, and sometimes, oddly, whole warrens of rabbits would be crossing. Needless to say, we ate well when this happened. Birds were flying away screeching warnings as they went. The fact was that nature was telling us to flee west. We knew what they were fleeing. The plague was quickly taking over eastern Ireland. Regardless, we continued forward traveling northeast towards Dublin. Our suspicions were confirmed the next morning after only a couple of hours of travel.

We came across one of the gray creatures unexpectedly and almost ran over the poor beast as we did not see it crouched low as it feasted on a rabbit that it too had captured with ease. We backed the horses away as they almost threw us with the smell of decay and sickness that the creature put off. We were all able to stay horsed as the creature, with madness, realized that we were near. She was probably thirty years old and must have had a rough life before her death. She was in a ripped and dirty brown dress with an equally disheveled apron that half hung off of her body and was covered in the gore of her lunch.

I had already nocked an arrow to the string of my longbow as she screamed and shambled towards us. The sound was excruciating as her pitch reached a fevered high. She snarled as she could sense the closeness of her prey. I drew and fired without second thought. It had only been a couple of weeks since we had even been introduced to this plague and already I put the afflicted down without remorse. I guess that was the trade off after having to kill so many in the village only two days before. They lost their humanity. They were not the villagers they had once been, and it was now us or them.

Edward dismounted to confirm my kill. I had hit her in the middle of her snarling mouth as she attacked us. Sean held Edward's horse steady, but we could tell that the smell of death and blood had almost panicked them. I thought perhaps it had been Fang's battle growl that had scared the horses, but Fang was calm and now stood beside Edward as if protecting him as he walked towards the beast. The horses were battle trained to not scare at the clash of sword on shield, death, and blood, but they were spooked here more than I had ever seen them before. Edward said a prayer for the poor woman and put her apron over her face after moving her off of the road, a sad and unworthy burial.

As he walked back to us, Fang went prone with his ears flat against his head and he growled deep in his chest. Edward was able to get his axe off of his shoulder to stop the first creature that came out of the bushes on the side of the path near the body of the dead woman. He decapitated it with a single practiced stroke. I nocked another arrow as

Sean dismounted still holding the reins of both horses in a single hand as he drew his hammer with the other.

We did not see the two creatures come in behind the horses for we had noticed the low moan and the sounds of many shuffling feet from up the road ahead of us. I turned toward the noise as Fang barked a warning. There must have been over twenty creatures coming down the road towards us. Somehow, we had managed to miss their approach with the attack of the one woman. Sean turned to grab the crossbow Sir Walter had given him.

As he did so, the beast behind his horse bit into the horse's flank panicking both of the horses that Sean was holding on to. The horse reared and kicked out behind it taking the creature in the face. The horses bolted up the road in fright straight into the coming horde. They barreled over the top of Sean but Edward was able to get out of their way. Edward put down the other creature behind us with his sling-shot and turned to help Sean back to his feet. The horse's kick had taken care of the other creature and Sean although bruised and covered in mud, was unharmed.

We watched in horror as the horses crashed into the coming swarm of creatures. They surrounded the poor beasts and pulled them down. The sound that the horses made as they were attacked was miserable and frightening. I had to call Fang back as he ran towards the chaos. If they would attack the horses, then they might attack Fang, and I would not risk that for anything.

I dismounted and tied my horse to a tree beside the road

commanding Fang to guard what was now our only horse. Sean had been able to free his crossbow from one of the horses before they bolted, but only grabbed three bolts. The three of us moved forward, stalking the feeding horde who was currently too preoccupied to notice our approach.

As soon as he was in range, Sean dropped one creature with the crossbow, missing a second, and taking another in the chest. Edward began on the outside hitting the creatures that were still standing trying to reach the struggling horses. I moved to the right and up a small bank on the side of the road. There I fired at the one small opening on the closest horse in between the arms and legs of its attackers. I pulled my arm down as I fired to pull the arrow down. It struck the horse in the chest and it ceased to fight.

I'm not sure if the creatures lost interest in eating the horse now that it was dead, or if they finally realized they were not alone, but several broke off from the feast and headed our way. Sean stood below me on the road; he would protect me as I dropped as many of the creatures as I could from above him. Edward would join him when he ran out of ammunition. I wasn't able to kill another horse as the first creatures reached Sean and I turned my attention to our immediate danger. Sean screamed in fury as he crashed his hammer down on the first creature to him.

Unfortunately, his battle cry served as bait to the other creatures and they scrambled over each other to come for us. Edward fired another two shots with his slingshot before reaching behind him and pulling his shield and then axe free as he stepped to Sean's left flank.

I noticed that there were way too many creatures as they began to leave the horses. I turned and whistled for Fang and watched as Sean stepped forward raining crushing blows down on his attackers.

Edward was rushed by three of the creatures. He bashed the first in the face with his shield as it came from his left, ducked under the arms of another coming from his right; he then bought his axe up in an underhanded blow straight into the neck of the third in front of him. He twisted to the right in a backhand swing cutting half through the neck of the one he had stepped past on his right and twisting and bringing his shield rim down on the open mouth of the first he had knocked down.

I shot one of my few remaining arrows just over his shoulder as he stood and shot a creature as it came up from behind him. I hit it in the arm, but the arrow checked its speed enough for Edward to turn and meet it.

I heard a moan behind me as I fired my last two arrows in a group moving towards Sean hitting one in the eye and another in the shoulder. I turned with my bow up to have anything between me and my invisible assailants. There were two creatures behind me. I threw my bow into the legs of the first tripping it as I drew Oíche to hack at its reaching hands. I felt the other creature grab my shoulder as I did so and fear gripped me as it wrenched me backwards. It would have gotten me if eighty pounds of fur had not collided with it at that moment.

Fang had come straight to me after I called him, and he had saved my life. He tore the throat out of the creature and did not stop until it stopped moving. I stood and killed the one I had tripped as it raised itself up onto its knees.

I called Fang as I headed down the small slope to join my friends who were being hard pressed by ten creatures. Fang went right, wide around the creatures, and came in behind the ones farthest back, biting at ankles and tripping and slowing as many as he could. Sean's hammer was a blur as he struck heads with the spiked end of the hammer, and then twisting it lightning fast in his hands to push another creature back. I called out to them as I rushed in between them so they would know I was there and not think me an assailant in their blood rush.

At first, it was if the creatures did not know I was there. They were so focused on Sean and Edward that I was able to dance in and out of my comrades' fights and pick apart the back ranks of their attackers. We had thinned the horde considerably, but we were also tiring quickly. Edward still faced two creatures, Sean another three, and I had one rather large creature headed my way. He must have been a miller or a blacksmith because he was huge.

He crushed another creature that got in his way of me and stalked forward with a drooping mouth, a moan, and a determination to feed. I parried his first swing of a massive arm with Oíche, cutting tendon and bone like butter. He howled but slugged me with his other hand in response. I reeled from the hit and blood obscured the vision in my left eye. Fang charged in behind the man and latched on to the back of his thigh slowing him just enough for me to regain my balance. Fang then took a huge swat himself and yipped in pain before charging back in to bite the same thigh.

I slashed down cutting off the creature's arm as it reached back at Fang. I then buried Oíche in its chest, foolishly thinking that this would faze it at all. I retracted the sword and stepped back. The creature swung at me again and again making my arms go numb at the endless barrage. As I felt my strength leaving me, I heard a sickening thud as Sean's hammer took the creature in the chest stopping its advance, and there was then a spray of blood as Edward swung his axe with all his remaining strength at the creature's neck, then stepped forward and punched out hard with his shield to topple the creature over Fang who jumped for the thing's ankles at the precise moment when needed. Once it was down, Sean was able to put it down with a giant's blow to the head.

The three of us collapsed from exhaustion and Fang came over to me and started licking his paws as if nothing had happened. Sean, watching the dog, began to laugh uncontrollably so that tears came into his eyes, and for a lack of anything else to do, Edward and I joined him. We were now down three horses, supplies, and beyond tired, but we counted and realized that the four of us had just killed over thirty creatures. I went back and fetched my horse and knowing we did not have the strength or will to bury these poor souls, we continued up the king's road on foot leading one warhorse and being led by one hell of a good dog.

Chapter 18

We walked for over an hour before we stopped to rest. We ate a very meagre mouthful of food out of my saddlebag and contemplated our next move. We knew that we now had very little food and few supplies, but luckily for us we had our weapons and armor. We loaded some of the weapons and armor onto my horse and then we continued on with a slightly lighter step. We knew we needed to find a safe place to spend the night and preferably somewhere we could get more horses and supplies.

Edward chimed in as we started walking back up the road, " lads, there must be another village not far up the king's road. We just need to hope and pray to the good lord that the village has not been lost." Sean's eyes got a glassy look to them as he thought about a possible village, "Yes" he said, "one with a tavern, and ale, and food. Lots of food!" I answered him, "The day is quickly passing. We do not have the time to hope for somewhere today. We need to find a place to defend. That horde was not that far back. We cannot assume that we are safe."

The afternoon was waning quickly. We continued walking, afraid to stop, not knowing what the night would hold for us. We felt safer moving unless we could find somewhere easily defensible. So, we walked. A light rain started which would have been fine except it didn't stop. The rain continued for the next hour and it started to slow us down. The road was turning into mud and my boots were beginning to get more stuck with each step I took.

Edward spoke up after the horse slipped in the mud and almost fell into him, "we must find shelter. The horse is going to break a leg and then we'll all be lost." He was right. We did not have a choice. We had come a few hours up the road since the attack where we lost our horses and we could feel like we had gone far enough that any close at the time would not be catching up to us. We stopped under a tree to decide what we should do next. A small path turned away from the road and we assumed that that path would lead to either a village or to at least some kind of shelter in order for a path to be worn out on the way to the main road.

I turned to Fang and dropped to a knee. He licked my face and I scratched behind his ears. "Fang, check out down the path and see if there is anywhere for us to shelter for the night. Shelter, Fang."

I pointed down the path and he took off giving us a playful bark. We ate some dried fish out of the saddle bags and hoped that Fang would find somewhere to get us out of the rain. Thirty minutes passed and Fang suddenly reappeared next to us, spooking the horse a little as he appeared out of the rain. He spun around three times as if chasing his tail and barked and then took off back down the small trail.

We packed up and quickly followed him hoping that his keen nose had found something besides the muck, and the mud, and the rain. We walked down the path and it seemed as if it had been little used of late. I began to worry that the trail would lead nowhere. After walking for what seemed like forever, the path left the marshy fields and entered the forest.

Fang barked to make sure we would continue to follow him and we did. We were hoping beyond hope that we were not headed toward a plague ravaged village. We were wet, miserable, and irritable. Sean had begun to groan and sigh regularly, and I could see that Edward was starting to drag. When it seemed as if we could go no further, we stopped in a clearing and looked around. The rain was falling at a quickened pace and we were in for a horrible night with little sleep.

Suddenly, from the far side of the clearing, a voice greeted us. "Well, what 'ave we 'ere. Wee knights in the muck seeing how long it'll take em to rust all the way through. Lads, I'm afraid that you're going to get a bit moldy around the ears if you're gonna stay in the wet like this."

He was a small man, and very old, bundled beneath a thick black and grey cloak with holes bitten into it from moths and heavy use. "Come with me, sir knights, and I'll get ye dry and warm, and give ye a chance to clean up a bit. The name is Mordecai, and you can call me that or Cai, whichever ye prefer young masters."

We followed him for a lack of anything else to do. We were exhausted and the thought of having a dry place to sleep tonight and a chance to clean the gore off of our gear and sharpen our weapons next to a fire was about the best thing we had ever heard.

"Got some fresh venison cooking over the fire, lads," he said.

… And then that was the best thing we had ever heard.

CHAPTER 19

Mordecai had been living in an area locally known as Kilkenny for the last forty years. He had originally been from an area on the southern border of the Kingdom of France which was past England on the mainland. He had come to Ireland on a mission of the Catholic Church to help tame the Pagan Irish. Unfortunately for him, St. Patrick had come six hundred years before him and most of our country except for in the wild, out-of-the-way places had already converted to Christianity and he could not find anyone to tame, at least not anyone who would let him try to tame them.

So, he had met a nice Irish gal, fallen in love, and then lost her some fifteen years before we met him. He decided upon her death to move into the wild as his original mission had asked of him and so he had come here and lived ever since. He spent much of his time talking and preaching to travelers on the road from the southern kingdom to the north, and had stayed reasonably out of trouble and out of sight.

He had a small hovel backed up against some rocks on the edge of the forest, and the Suir River ran not too far away and that provided him with food when he could not get any by hunting. After coming in out of the rain, we took off our wet clothes and hung them to dry, and he served us large skewers of roasted venison. We tore into it hungrily because we were exhausted and had had nothing but salted beef and fish for the last week.

Grease dribbled from our chins as we ate and Mordecai was generous with his food. We ate until our stomachs were full, and even then we ate a little more. Mordecai had taken care of our horse as we ate and as he came back in he threw another log on the fire as we all sat back and put our feet up. He pulled out a long tobacco pipe out of his robe and began to smoke as he looked us over.

"Well, lads. You share your news with me, and I'll share my news with ye. That seems like a more than fair arrangement if I do say so myself, and I do." He laughed at his own rhyme and we could not help but smile.

Edward and Sean deferred to me as the official spokesman of our group so I sat up and tried to think of how to start. "Well, master Cai, I'm not sure what you know about the current state of Ireland, so I do not know what to tell you, and what you might already know. Do you know of the current plague that is beginning to ravage Ireland?"

Mordecai's eyebrows raised and in the midst of his heavily wrinkled face was a smirk that said he knew much more than he was going to tell us. He answered "I know a little of something and a lot of nothing. So, Sir Banion, why don't you tell me what is going on in our fair land."

I was slightly taken aback at his words but pressed on

explaining everything that Sir Walter had told us of the plague and its movement across Europe. I shared our experiences on the road, Sir Walter leaving us, the wins, and the very recent loss of our horses and gear. Mordecai listened with a serious interest. He harrumphed at all the right points, showed surprise, and seemed angry at the loss of the horses. His face grew worried as we told him our fears of what would be ahead on the road and what we expected to be waiting for us in Dublin.

Finally, after what seemed like hours, I leaned back and waited for him to explain to us all what we should do next. He looked at us each in turn, showing a kindness in his eyes that would be unexpected from a stranger, and then he spoke: "Lads, you have overcome much in a very short amount of time. In fact, you have handled yourselves with honor and bravery in circumstances that most men could not deal with in their entire lives. You have done well, but I will not lie to you and tell you that you near your goal or that it will get easier. In fact, boys, your story is just getting started, and you are not going to make it to Dublin soon."

He stared at us, and we stared at him. I don't know if he was waiting for a reaction for us, or, in shock, if we had no reaction to give. Sean guffawed after a few tense moments and the tension was immediately broken. We gave uneasy glances at one another and Edward kindly invited Mordecai to explain what he meant. We all had subconsciously moved to the edge of our seats.

"The storm has gone ahead of you, Sir Knights. Whereas it seemed like you were just hearing of the plague when

Walter came to Cork, the waves were already crashing on the rest of the country. You have been too long in the wild and have missed the goings on in the rest of Éire. You must not go to Dublin next, it will be too messy there anyway, but you must head into the West Country.

Walter will not have been able to warn everyone, and there are rumors of uprisings and evil things happening already amongst the men of the west. Rumors tell of famine from earlier in the year which will lead men to take this present plague as an opportunity to get what they want. Think on your duty as knights of Ireland. Your father, Banion, did not just send you to Dublin to kneel before your uncle, he sent you there to offer aid and succor to the people of Ireland in trying times. Think on what I have said, and we'll talk later. Either way, you will have to be off in the morning to continue your quest in whichever direction it leads ye."

And with that, Mordecai walked out of his hut. Perhaps he went to make sure all of the land around his home was safe. Perhaps he went to set traps for the creatures now roaming the roads of Ireland as he told us he had done. Undoubtedly though, he left so that we would have to make our own decisions as men. A decision that we were unsure how to make.

Edward began our debate, "yer father gave us a task. The king sent us to Dublin. That is where we should be heading and nowhere else. It is our duty to follow his orders. We are his knights."

"But our duty is to the kingdom. Not just to be errand boys." Sean replied. "If knights of Ireland are needed in the west, then it is our duty to be where injustice lurks. Also, we are surely guaranteed a right royal fight headin' into danger like we will no doubt be."

Edward rejoined, "So we just give up the task set before us then? And what would the king say? 'You lads couldn't even finish your first charge? Way to change yer minds haf way through and gallop off after a fight.'"

The heat was rising on Sean's face, and I could see the explosion coming as the two of them were both passionate men. I decided it was best if I took hold while I still had a chance.

"Sean, Edward, listen." I said. "Both of you speak honorably about we three fulfilling our duty to the king and our country, and both of you are right. We need to get word to the king and make sure that the King's peace, whatever may be left of it, is upheld in the west. With this new danger, we cannot be at war with ourselves. There are many that will take this opportunity to forgo custom and law and see revenge on those they deem have wronged them."

As we sat and discussed, Mordecai came back into the hut. He had, in his hands, a rolled parchment. "Rider on the road." He said as he came in, handed the roll to me, and then busied himself around the fire. I glanced at the seal and saw that it was fixed with the high king's mark. I broke the seal and read the words on the page.

To all my royal brothers:
Dublin has been overrun by demon possessed men.
A plague has come to our shores which threatens
To end our fair country. I, along with
my knights, have ridden westward
Toward Galway to regroup and plan
On how to fight the devil's wicked minions.
Signed
His Royal Majesty and High King of Ireland
Patrick O'Kelly

"That settles it then." Edward announced after I had passed the letter around. "We head west. That way we can check into the rumors of trouble in the western counties and then meet up with the king and complete our mission from your father, Banion."

And so it was decided. We ate a hearty dinner with Mordecai, he blessed us and promised to pray for us, and then we went to sleep knowing that in the morning we would be back on the path that God had set before us.

CHAPTER 20

The sun rose the following morning with a faint red glare. This most likely predicted bad weather later in the day as we remembered from the old Bible rhyme "Red sky at night, sailors' delight. Red sky at morning, sailors take warning." Mordecai woke us with a gentle touch and had prepared for us all new packs with food enough for a week in each. He had been drying and salting fish and beef for weeks after realizing the coming hunger of both the creatures and we humans. It was a rich gift in a soon to be harder time, but he would not allow us to leave any or pay for it.

He also drew a crude map which showed a narrow road leaving the main highway to Dublin. He explained that this was the most promising route into the West Country and he also explained how many people we should expect to see, how often we would come across a village, and where we might buy horses. He had taken good care of us, and we parted with the promise that we would see him again, and pass on the kindness he had showed us to others.

We spent the morning circling Mordecai's swamp. We looked for stray creatures and were able to put down quite a few that could have caused trouble for him over the coming week. We then continued up the road for a few hours without incident, and clearly saw the path which we were to take west. We looked up and down the road for sign of anyone dead or alive, and saw no one. So, off we went.

Mordecai had explained that we would not reach the first village on this path for two days. Therefore, that night, we found a nice bit of high ground, nestled into the rocks of a long abandoned fort of the old people, and slept without issue. Fang went off into the night and returned at dawn with a bloody muzzle. I was glad that he was able to find game so easily. There might be hope yet. It had rained during the night, but our protective rocks kept most of it off of us. We allowed the horse to graze for a bit as we prepared breakfast, and then set off again.

We reached the town of Fernwood at midday on the second day away from Mordecai. The windows were boarded up, and it was obvious that the townsfolk had planned on making their village look deserted. However, the novelty of three knights walking into the village caused mayhem for their plans. The first few little boys ran out to see us, and we laughed as their groaning parents came out and scolded them for not staying hidden.

The town elders came to us and begged for information. We were able to share the news of what has come to our emerald shores, and in turn, they put us up for the night. A grizzled old knight named Sir Stephan put us up in his decaying hall. He had fought in the civil war that my father and uncle had been victorious in thirty years before. He regaled us with stories of my father and his battle prowess as a young knight around our age. His tired, wrinkled face stretched into animation that it had not seen in years as he recounted the exploits of the great knights of Ireland. He even declared loudly that he had once met King Arthur while visiting Cornwall with the Lady Iseult's father, but he was not near old enough to have been in such history.

Our dinner was interrupted by some of the men of the village who sought more answers than we had given earlier. They demanded to know the king's response and wanted to know when the army would be here to defend their village. It was heartbreaking to have to tell them that we did not know how well our country was doing, but we were able to help them plan defenses and teach them how to fight off the creatures that would surely again threaten their doors.

We stayed in Fernwood for two days working with the men to build obstacles and traps. In exchange for this work and our support, Sir Stephan gave us his old warhorse, and the village was able to give us another one. It got the three of us back on horseback and that meant that our quest would be able to continue at a much quicker pace.

We put the village behind us with the promise to not forget them, and we almost had to tie Sir Stephan to his chair to keep him from coming with us. The thought of a quest had filled an emptied part of his soul, and he wanted to be young again and to fight for Ireland. It was only our earnest desire that he stay and lead the defense of Fernwood that finally allowed us to leave him. His courage was a testament to his honor as a knight, and though he might be forgotten in the stories of our time, he would remain ever present in our thoughts when the three of us were called on to have courage.

CHAPTER 21

On horseback, the mood of our party had completely changed. The three of us felt like we were finally back on track to continue our quest, and we felt like we were honoring the king by helping his people. It had almost been two full days of travel without seeing one of the creatures and we were getting too comfortable as we traveled without incident. In the afternoon, Sean began to tell us a story:

"Once upon a time," he began, "there lived a French knight by the name of Sir Henri de Troyes. Henri loved fancy food. He loved it so much that he was constantly seen eating by all the townspeople that lived near his manor. He would come down into the village each day with his personal chef and pick out the best that was offered for his own table. The people began to call him Henri la Faim which means Henry the hungry. Henri would send his men at arms on quests to find him exotic and delicious food, and they brought him back rare food for his table.

Henri, later in his life, began to get quite fat. He got to the point where he could not mount his horse and he would have to have servants help him bathe and dress each day. He could no longer do his knightly duties on his own, but because of the service he had shown the king early in his life, he continued to live in prosperity. However, all good things must come to an end. A great famine swept through the countryside of France and this was followed by a long and brutally cold winter. Henri had plenty of food stocked up for himself, but, as the winter continued, his people began to look to him for aid. It was his duty as a lord to take care of the people who worked his land. However, Henri's greed and gluttony had developed too far over the years to allow him to think of offering any of his precious food to the people. It was food fit for a king after all, not food meant to be tasted by the lower orders.

The people, watching their children starve, finally had enough. They stormed Henri's keep and beat on the doors to his bedroom door. His own men did not try to resist because they too were in hunger. Henri, scared, commanded the people to stop and even as he did so he stuffed his face to the point of fill. They heard him speak through his chewing and this enraged the people even farther. They burst into Henri's chambers and pounced upon him. They tore him apart and began to eat everything in sight. The whole village, it is said, feasted in the room of Henri de Troyes that day.

When the people had eaten their fill, they decided to put Henri on trial for not taking care of them. They searched his chambers but Henri was not to be found. They searched the entire castle, high and low for any sign of where Henri had gone. It surprised them because he was such a large man, and not very quick anymore, but they couldn't find him. Finally, a cry from his chambers rushed them all back to where their feast began.

There, underneath the table, was a large, rather fat,

hand holding a fork in a death grip. It had been ripped off and there were bite marks where the wrist would have connected. It slowly dawned on the people of Troyes that their hunger and anger had led them to do something they would never escape. They had eaten Henri la Faim. Sickened with themselves, the townspeople held a burial for what was left of Henri, his hand. The steward sent a letter saying that Henri had died of natural causes, and the whole village swore to never tell a soul what had happened during the winter of famine."

It was at this point that Edward began to laugh. Not just a snicker, but loud uncontrollable laughter at Sean's story. In between gasps he managed, "if they promised to keep it a secret, then how do we know the story?"

Sean looked rather perplexed having never really thought of this before, and started to respond but I interrupted him, " Sean, why did you tell us this story? hahaha! Is it one that yer ma told ye when you were a wee lad who wouldn't leave the dinner table?"

Edward gasped in desperation trying to stay on his horse as his laughter continued. Sean took a hearty swing at Edward from his own horse while yelling over his shoulder at me, "It's because I am hungry, and I will eat one of you if we do not stop for supper! Edward is first on the menu!" We all laughed at his response as he took off after Edward. They circled me a few times, Edward to escape, and Sean to catch his prey.

An ear splitting scream interrupted the chase, and we all

three instinctively drew our weapons. It erupted again off the path in front of us to our left, and it was clearly the terrified scream of a young girl. Not knowing what to expect, and after a cautious glance at one another, we left the path in search of the source of the scream. Fang ran ahead and we followed him towards an upcoming clearing.

The source of the scream found us before we found her. As we rode into a clearing, the brush on the other side began to rustle. It was obvious that something was coming. What we saw next was close to unbelievable. A little girl burst into the clearing startling the horses. She stopped with an expression of awe and surprise at having run into us. Her mouth gaped open and an exasperated "huh?" came out of her mouth. She immediately burst into tears, and Edward jumped down and caught her in his arms.

Suddenly, Fang growled a warning as the reason for her screams soon became apparent when one of the creatures came shambling into the clearing after her. Sean turned and put an armored boot directly into its face snapping its head back. It fell lifeless to the ground. The girl shivered and shuttered as Edward wrapped an extra blanket we had gotten from Mordecai around her. She was perhaps twelve years old, although she could have been younger. We left the clearing with the girl in Edward's arms. She whimpered quietly as we made our way back to the main road.

The lackadaisical attitude that we had as we had ridden without impediment was gone quickly. Sean and I fanned out to the front and sides of Edward, circling him as we made our way up the road. We took turns scouting the path ahead, and it was Sean that came back declaring he had found a good place to rest for the night. He had found what must have been some lost watchtower along this path to the west. It was in a crumbling ruin, but the ruin still managed to have somewhat of a low wall around it. This would provide us with some cover if the creatures caught up to us at all.

We made camp and risked lighting a fire. The girl was still shivering. Whether it was from the cold or from the fear we could not surmise. Edward sat near her as we ate and tried to get her to talk. She dozed off after dinner and the three of us whispered together at the recent turn of events.

"We do not know who she is or where she is from?" Sean started. "True enough." I replied, "But that doesn't change the fact that we have accepted responsibility for her now."

Edward added, "But what then? Do we take her with us until we find the king? Do we drop her off with the first people we come across? We cannot expect to find someone caring enough to not abuse her as soon as we leave her with them."

"But," I entreated. "We cannot really take her with us for the rest of our quest. We do not have the resources, and we are almost guaranteed a fight. We cannot protect her then."

Sean replied, "We could take her to Fernwood. They would take her in and give her a life worth living." Edward scoffed, "yeah, but we cannot guarantee that they are safe either. Hell, we cannot even be sure that Fernwood is still standing since we were there three days ago."

We all fell into a stony silence and contemplated our fate as the protectors of another person. The responsibility weighed on us, and the desire to make a good decision was present before us. Sean and Edward deferred to my status for the decision, and I could not help thinking that a few short weeks ago all I could think about was whether or not I would be able to pass the trials.

"Well boys, I think we need to hear what she has to say for herself. Might be that she has help nearby and we just need to get her back to family or friends safely."

Sean then said the obvious thing that I was trying to avoid, "then why is she out here being chased by one of those things?"

"Because I had to get away!" The girl interrupted. She had woken up without us noticing and had probably been listening as we debated our next move. "Get away from what?" Edward asked. She had taken to Edward after he had rescued her, and she could not help but stare at him. "M'name's Molly. I'm from Shannon. It's a small village on the river not far from here. Those things came and Da told me to run as he and the boys went to fight 'em off. I don't know what happened then, but I ran here. I've an aunt in Fernwood and thought to make it to her."

She seemed to be telling the truth and, after a look at the map that Mordecai had given us, we realized that we couldn't be more than a day's ride from Shannon.

"I'm dead worried about da and the boys and the rest of the village." I wondered why she hadn't made it farther from the village, and so I asked when the attack had happened. Molly replied with "yesterday marnin. I was bringin' in the milk when Patty came running up and told me to get to Da. Da had a stave in his hand and a look o' fear on his face like I ne're seen. He told me to run to aunties so I did."

I began to mull over what she had said. I looked at Sean who looked worried and slightly confused. I wondered if he too felt it weird that she hadn't made it farther. Edward answered for us before I could fully grasp all the potential of the situation. "We will take you back to Shannon. If the village is safe, then yer Da will be glad to know that you are okay."

The girl seemed relieved at this news, and Edward looked to me and Sean for confirmation. We nodded, but something just did not seem right about this whole thing. Molly had settled back in and quickly fell asleep again. Sean and Edward did as well after I told them I would take first watch. I sat up with Fang and contemplated the unnatural speed of this plague and what might be waiting for us in Shannon the next day.

CHAPTER 22

It was a cold, damp morning when Sean woke us up as dawn slowly crept up like a stalking lioness. We ate a rather boring bit of dried meat as we prepared the horses and scouted the road ahead. Molly continued to ride with Edward, and we used our leap frog formation from the day before to keep the way ahead safe. If we did not run into trouble, we should arrive at the village of Shannon right before nightfall.

This presented us with two issues. If the village had succeeded in repelling the dangerous creatures, then it would be great to stay in the village tonight and eat a warm meal next to a fire. If, however, the village had been overrun, then it would be beyond foolish to try to get anywhere near it without direct sunlight to make our path and enemies clear. It was thoughts like these that occupied my time as we rode.

There were several instances when we came across stray creatures. This was not an encouraging sign as most of them probably came from the village itself. We had to bypass a whole group of them at one point. We were not quite stealthy enough to avoid their detection, but we were able to get past. Several of the group turned and followed after us. We would have to put some distance between us and them if we wanted to avoid a fight.

Having Molly with us changed the group dynamic. We would probably have quickly dispatched any creatures we came across had it just been we three boys, but we could not risk Molly's safety. It was hard to ride past and know that we were leaving a danger near the road. This danger could cause problems for our countrymen, and I felt a tinge of shame at the thought of not completely doing my job. The job that Sir Walter had given us.

The afternoon light was failing as we came upon the outskirts of the village. There was no one to be found as we started crossing the fields. There was just enough light that we could see a good distance ahead of us. We could see smoke ahead near the village center and hoped with all our might that they were burning bodies of the fallen creatures, and that it was not the village itself beginning to burn. I drew Oíche and held her low on my right side as we rode into the village. Sean, too, prepared himself for a fight just in case. I saw Edward, out of the corner of my eye, loosen the haft of his axe where it hung on his belt.

We came around the corner as we passed the first buildings and made for the village square. There was no sign of life as we entered, but this had been the case in Fernwood as well. The really weird thing was that there was not one bark from a dog as we entered the village.

Usually, three horse riding knights would cause such a clamor in a village that all the dogs of the village would freak out in warning to their owners. We heard no sound. We entered the square ready for anything. A smouldering fire still burnt, but there was no one there tending it. We circled the fire looking for any signs.

Unexpectedly, Molly jumped off of the back of Edward's horse and screamed at the top of her lungs: "NOW!!!"

With surprise we all turned and saw her sprint off in between the blacksmith's shop and the farrier's. At her signal the buildings erupted all around us, and very dirty men and women armed with all kinds of crude and sadistic looking weapons emerged and started to surround us. They had all covered their faces, arms, and legs with mud and it gave them a fierce look. Many had dark red mud covering their jaws and this looked distinctly like blood.

The three of us backed carefully into each other forming a small circle from which one of us could look in each direction and Fang bared his teeth and moved to my side. A large man holding what really looked like a human forearm walked forward and the crowd moved aside as he came. He walked directly towards the three of us. I balanced Oíche across the pommel of my horse and nocked an arrow to my longbow drawing the cord halfway, and making the intent clear that he had come quite close enough.

He looked at the broadhead on the end of my arrow and let forth a booming laugh. " HAHAHA! What are you going to do wee knight, shoot us all?" The crowd around him laughed alongside him and leaned eagerly forward to see how we would react.

"All of you?" I said, "No, not all of you. But you, big man, will die first, and I can guarantee that." I grinned with what I hope was a look that said "try me." He did not seem amused at my response and growled for two of his men. He signaled for them and told them to "take away my little bow." They came forward eagerly but were met by Sean sliding off his horse and stepping in front of me. His natural size and strength came into perspective and the two men checked their advance as Sean swung his warhammer in front of him in a wide arc.

The leader howled and this encouraged them forward. Sean struck first sending his hammer directly out in front of him and sending the head directly into the first attacker's face. There was a loud snap as his nose was crushed back into his head. Sean followed with an overhead swing that blasted through the second man's neck and demolished his spine in a splitting crunch. Sean stepped back as if daring anyone else to come forward.

The death of his men enraged the leader of the town, and I knew there was little we could do now to avoid even more confrontation. His face was contorted in rage and spit flew from his lips as he began to approach us. He, with a look of pure menace in his eyes, calmly declared "That was not a very good way to treat your hosts. We plan on having you for dinner much like any travelers that come this way." He laughed and took a bite out of the arm he seemed to be holding. The townsfolk snickered and began to chant in a rhythmic fashion, and Fang began to growl and howl.

"Have them for dinner. Have them for dinner. Just like our friends, we'll have them for dinner."

This they repeated and the crowd began to get quite agitated. Then we heard the moan. We saw one of the mud-covered townsfolk rush to open the door to the main hall and out of it came a dozen of the creatures. The villagers backed away as the creatures shuffled into the dying light. One sniffed the air and seemed confused but with some precise shouting and urging of the villagers, the creatures began to come our way. The leader of the village sang out with glee, "Start the feast for us brothers!"

Edward was the first to break from the shock of all that was happening. We had obviously happened upon a wild group of clansmen who apparently had decided that, like the creatures, human flesh was the most enticing treat in these new times. As the cannibals began to circle us, Edward yelled "come on lads, no need to see what happens next!" I saw him stoop over and grab the reigns of Sean's horse. He began to turn towards the way we had come into the village but that way was blocked. In a second's time I made the decision. " West! To the west!"

Sean was keeping the growing horde of villagers and creatures at bay, and I had seen our chance. The road leaving the village to the west was the least heavily guarded. "Sean! Let's go!" Sean rushed forward instead, sliding towards the fire. He reached in and grabbed a huge tree bough. As he flung the branch at the nearest cottage roof, the villagers howled in anger. He reached back in and grabbed another, throwing it onto the roof of the main hall as he finally retreated back to the horses.

We started to speed up as we knew we would have to break through the villagers to get out. The first of the creatures were now running over where we had been moments before. We set the horses to a gallop, and Sean did not even try to mount his horse. He grabbed on to the pommel with one hand and ran alongside his horse, hopping to keep up with the pace.

Edward and I crashed into the first villagers, and I swung down hard with Oíche catching a man full in the face. Fang ran ahead and tackled the first man to step in our way with a weapon. There was a great snarling and snapping of Fang's teeth and a blood curdling scream that ended as quickly as it began. I saw Sean kick off a stone walkway and pull himself all the way onto his horse as Edward tossed back the reins and bashed a ferocious looking, crazed woman in the face with his shield. She dropped the spear she had been leveling at Sean in his moment of distraction and clutched at her face. The end of the village was in sight and there, standing to one side, was Molly. She smiled mischievously and waved. The guts of that girl!

We broke through to the edge of the village and the path entered the woods. It was quickly apparent as to why she had been smiling as we went that way when we then saw the path ahead choked with unthinking creatures. They noticed us as we noticed them, Fang barked a warning, and we were able to turn aside before being entirely surrounded by them. As we turned we saw that the villagers had run out of the village after us, hoping to catch us in between two dangers. By rare chance, I was able to see back up the road into the village and saw the woman screaming with the busted face be swarmed by the creatures from the village. Her screams adding to the smell of fresh blood must have attracted them to her. A sudden thought shook me, and I realized what we must to do survive. "Cut the villagers, it will attract the creatures! Leave them alive."

This was one of the weirdest commands I had ever given, and I would have never thought that such words would ever escape my lips. Sean and Edward seemed to understand as we turned back to the village. The village leader was standing directly in the middle of the road on the outskirts of town and glaring at us with a tense ferocity. My first arrow hit him full in the chest. It knocked him back several steps, but he managed to keep his feet with a look of sheer confusion on his face followed by a look of extreme rage. He bellowed out in pain and anger, and my second arrow hamstrung him and dropped him to his knees. I could see the blood pouring out as he dropped onto all fours.

Sean swung low and caught whoever he could with a bone mangling blow dropping them onto the path in between us and the now incensed mob of creatures coming from the woods. Edward too was slashing left and right with his ax, hitting whatever he could. Here an arm, here a shoulder, here a chest. It was brutal work. Fang leapt to and from wherever he could find a target. He bit and scratched and moved on often before his victim knew he was there. Our plan, although one of the most brutal strategies we would have ever imagined, seemed to be taking effect. The creatures were pouncing on the downed and bleeding villagers, and this gave us a chance to take off to the northwest of the village where gratefully we found a path and left this hellhole behind.

CHAPTER 23

We rode hard for almost two hours trying to put as much distance as we could between ourselves and the village of Shannon. The cries of the villagers as they were torn apart by the creatures they had apparently worshiped followed us into the woods and rang in our ears as we finally slowed down and had time to think.

The horses were exhausted having ridden all day and then been pushed hard in the midst of their own fear of what was surrounding them. It was full dark now and we had made it far enough away that we felt that any possible survivors bent on revenge would never be able to track us as far as we had gotten away. We found a dense thicket of trees and wound our way deep within them about thirty meters away from the main road. We would be able to hear any pursuers while staying hidden. We posted Fang at the entrance to our little sanctuary as a silent watcher.

We brushed down the horses, and chewed on some hard salt beef as we fell warily down on our packs. We didn't dare light a fire, but the moon was bright and would allow us to not get snuck up on. We, under roughspun blankets that Mordecai had given us, dutifully saw to our weapons as fatigue threatened to overcome us. We cleaned off the blood, scraped away the muck, and sharpened the blades. I hated the fact that I had not been able to reclaim my arrows from the town leader's body. I had a finite amount and did not know when I would be able to get more.

One by one we finished our work and dropped off into an unpleasant sleep. My dreams were plagued by images of the villagers and their howling mad faces. I wondered how they had gone into such a feral reaction of the world in such a short amount of time. The whole village, too, had been a part. Sure, there might have been those against the eating of human flesh, but those dissenters might have been the first victims. If they had run out of food as a community why would they have not sought help from others? Or did they think this plague was the end of the world and so they might as well give in to the deep, dark desires of their flesh.

I woke up to see Fang in the moonlight sitting on Sean's chest. Sean woke up with a start, realized his lack of breath was caused by a fully grown wolf on top of him, shoved Fang off grumbling, and then rose and took his turn as sentry. Fang came over to me, licked my hand, and curled up next to me.

My dreams continued with Molly. It was painful to think that such a seemingly innocent girl had knowingly tricked those who were doing nothing more than trying to return her to her lost family. Her face morphed into the woman's face whom Edward had hit with his shield, and, as her scream pierced my ears, the face changed again into the undying yawn of a creature trying to sink its teeth into me. I woke up right as it would have bitten me and saw Edward shaking me gently.

"Your turn mate." He said, "Dawn is only a couple of hours

away."

I rose, grabbed my sword and left to get a good vantage point of the road. I wasn't there long when Fang came out of the darkness and lay down at my feet. His company was reassuring and I felt safe. I was still puzzled at the people of Shannon. Had these people been eating unwary travelers for longer than the plague had been around? Was it a part of some ancient religion requiring the consumption of human flesh?

There were old wives tales to such an effect but no one thought there was any merit to them. Mostly we thought they were told to us as children so that we would realize how good we had it. This was especially true, said our wet nurse, since the wild hill tribes had been eating each other when winters grew too cold and food was too scarce. I shuddered to think how close we had just been to death. The plague was not the only evil left in the world, and we, as knights, had a duty to stamp out such corruption and make Ireland safe for its people.

CHAPTER 24

The morning came slowly. It seemed that the stillness of the forest would never end. Yet, the birds began to sing as if they didn't have a care in the world. I took a short walk up the path in both directions making sure that we were alone and that there was not an ambush waiting for us in either direction. Fang made this true because his nose would have alerted me to anyone near us at all. I made my way back to camp and saw Sean saddling the horses as Edward bent over a small cook fire.

"I decided we needed something warm to eat after the last few days we have had," Edward said with care. He handed me a bowl of porridge and tipped some sausages in as well. He tossed Fang a few sausages as well, and we all sat around the small fire and ate. The effect of the warm food was almost immediate. The first smile I have had in what seemed like days crept onto my face as Sean let out a huge belch. We all had a laugh then, as Fang ate an extra sausage out of my hand as I had it headed towards my mouth. I chased him around the fire, but not really in anger.

Before leaving the area, Sean scratched our crude new danger symbol into a tree on the path. The snarling head over the cross. We wanted it to be clear that danger lay ahead if travelers were heading towards the village of Shannon. We finished packing up and headed back to the trail not long after that. We walked alongside the horses to give them a small break after having ridden them hard the day before. It felt good to stretch our legs too after being in the saddle for most of the week.

We had all donned part of our armor before leaving the camp. It must have been the sense of being completely surrounded by enemies now that most kept us on our guard. We each were wearing our mail that covered our torsos and upper arms. We had the lower vambrace to cover our forearms, and grieves to cover our legs. Wearing any more than this would have worn us out much too quickly so we left much of our armor on the horses. We needed an extra horse to carry our armor so that the warhorses did not have to act as pack animals in addition to their role in battle. It made them less effective in a fight to be carrying supplies attached to their back and sides. That would be something to take care of if we were given the chance, but all of us could feel the value of having good steel come between our bodies and the creatures' bites.

The morning was pretty uneventful as we continued to make our way west. We could not be but a few days ride from Galway where we might start hearing rumors of the king's whereabouts. We came to a split in the road early in the afternoon which put a stopper on our mirth. The split was not on Mordecai's map for us. There were no markers giving us any direction. There was only one thing that we could do. Split up. We would scout out the two different paths and see which one offered the best route for us. Fang and I took the path to the left, and Edward and Sean took the path to the right. We agreed to follow the path for half an hour, and then meet back up at the split in an hour.

It felt like a huge mistake to split up when we still did not fully grasp what we had to come up against, but it would take us twice as long to scout both paths as a group. Fang seemed to understand what we were doing and he ran up the road ahead of me. A scout, for the scout. I saw very little as I went up the path. I took a quick shot at a passing deer but missed. That would have really changed the way that we ate for the next few days and, in turn, our fortitude and stamina.

Fang came back periodically to almost check to see that I was still there. He would then disappear off to one side or the other of the trail for a few minutes. I had made it to around the time to return and, although I had not seen any signs telling me which direction I was going, I felt like it was safe for us to travel this way.

I whistled for Fang and turned back around. I hadn't gone more than a few minutes when I heard the pounding of hooves coming towards me. Fang's ears fell flat as we went off the path and around the side of a small tree covered hill for cover. Sean and Edward came bursting into view moments later and Sean had another horse in tow behind his. I called out to them as I saw Fang relax next to me. They reined up and came back towards me with looks of anxiety on their faces.

"Banion, thank God. We got here as soon as we could," Edward said as they both fought to catch their breath.
   "What happened to you two?" I asked with worry.

Sean nodded for Edward to continue as he turned around to face the way they had come.

Edward then began their story: "We hadn't gone but a couple of miles up the road when suddenly this horse came bolting up the path towards us. It looks like Sir Walter's horse and his supplies. As we grabbed the horse and tried to calm it from absolute panic, we wondered what the chances were that we had come across Walter's horse, and then that he must be near to us even then. As we talked the horse tried to bolt again and this was really weird.

We continued up the path looking for Sir Walter and the horse was straining against the reins trying to go back the way we had come. We were getting alarmed at its behavior and were getting ready to turn back when we heard the first moan. In seconds, the creatures were all around us having come out of the trees behind us as we came up. One grabbed at Sean, but all it got were greaves and then a swift kick in the face. We turned and ran, hoping that you had not run into similar difficulty. Banion, there must have been thirty of them freshly turned."

Even as he said these words uneasiness fell upon us all. We looked over our shoulders as if expecting creatures to burst from the tree line at any moment. After taking a moment to think of their story, I responded in the only way I knew how. I began to pray, thanking God that he had not allowed my two best friends to be taken away from me. If they hadn't returned, I would probably have set out after them and met a similar fate.

"The way ahead of us is clear. Let us shift some of our horses' burdens to Walter's horse and then put as much distance between us and them as we can before nightfall." We were quick to do this, and then set off back up the path that I had taken earlier. We whispered together at the thought of what had happened to Walter, and knew that if anyone could make it out of such a disaster, then it was him.

We put some good distance on the road that afternoon and began looking for a defensible position to wait out the night. We argued for some time about whether or not to stop or keep going, but finally we realized that we did not really know what was ahead of us and it would be better to not run into some major trouble exposed, at night. We were able to find a hillock with two steep sides. We tethered the horses on the steep side where they were less likely to face a danger. We started to set up a watch rotation before realizing that none of us would be able to sleep. So we sat up, in the dark, not risking a fire, and watched the coming darkness.

It was around midnight when Fang let out a low growl and positioned himself between us and the trees to the east. We saw movement in the moonlight, but could not make out what exactly it was. It felt like an eternity, but was probably not more than a few minutes, when a lone figure, stooping, in a cloak broke from the tree line and continued towards us. One of the horses whinnied loudly behind us at what could not have been a worse time. The shadowed figure stopped, and turned towards us. I had an arrow on my string already, hoping against hope that this was not the lead creature in the horde that Sean and Edward had run from earlier in the day.

We watched. The figure seemed to be listening for another sound. It did not really move like the creatures seemed to, and it seemed to be holding its arm at a weird angle to its chest. We had already discussed the need for stealth. We did not want to be discovered by anyone dead or alive in the darkness. Fang growled again. The figure started again, but this time was heading straight for us. I pulled the cord back on my bow halfway and waited, and watched.

The figure was taking a direct route to us like he knew exactly where we would be defending ourselves. He stumbled once or twice which worried me, and kept on. When he was about fifteen feet away I stood, drew the cord back to my ear, and shouted "HALT! Name yourself."

"Banion?" The man croaked as he fell to the earth. It registered with me what he had just said as Edward rushed past me towards the man. "Walter? Is that you?" Sean ran down to help Edward bring him up. I relaxed and called Fang to my side. "Fang, scout." I said as I pointed the direction that Walter had just come.

It took almost an hour to get Walter to the point where he could speak. We risked a fire and made him some hot tea and began to wash his wounds. Most were superficial and could have been caused by what must have been one hell of a rush through the woods to save his life. He had one cut on his upper back as if from a blade, but the worst came as we searched his legs. Halfway up his left calf was a serious tear that could only have been made with teeth. In fact, the markings showed without a doubt that the bite was from human teeth. A dog's bite would have been wider and more would have been torn away as it shook its head back and forth in a ripping fashion. Plus, Walter surely would have been able to dispatch one dog if it got to him, even at night.

We wrapped Walter in a blanket after tending to his wounds. We gave him some warm food and waited for him to tell us his tale. If we thought he was a bit skittish when we met him, when he was no one more than the strange knight looking uneasy at the trials, then we had no idea what he would be like later. He jumped at any noise, even when it was just us or the horses. He kept looking over his shoulders and off into the darkness, and there were a few times where he seemed to lose himself and then come back minutes later.

Walter finally worked up the fortitude and courage to tell us what had happened to him. He began, "Boys, I cannot believe our paths crossed again. Especially, in my time of most need. After we parted ways, I struck out to Killarney and intended to then make my way north and spread the word.

It was a few days after we split that I ran into my first creature. It was just a lone man. He was old, and must have been very poor. At first, I just thought he was a potato farmer judging by how grubby his clothes were, but, as I drew nearer, he lunged for me and the horse. Luckily, my horse, thank God you saved her, was battle trained and felt his attack coming and reared and kicked him full in the chest. The blow must have broken every bone in the thing's chest.

I slowed to watch, and it kept snapping at me even though it couldn't move anymore. I dispatched it and continued on. I reached Killarney after a week having run in to only the one creature. I thought that was a good sign, but also wondered how one lone creature had made it out into the middle of nowhere by itself.

As I reached the city, I was met by one of the local king's knights. He barred my path and asked whose business I was on. I declared that I had just come from yer father's court in Cork, and was on a mission for the high king himself. The knight did not believe me, and it would have come to blows if a herald had not ridden up at the moment and confirmed that they were waiting for a messenger from the king. I don't know if that was me or not, but I let them think it was. The city had walled themselves up. Apparently a ship had arrived the week before south of the city at a little harbor on the coast, and it was filled to the brim with an entirely infected crew from France.

They crashed into the harbor and were attacking people before they knew what hit 'em. Eventually, the king organized a defense of the castle and had quartered off the harbor and the surrounding sections of town. He was not going on the offense though because they had no idea what they were up against. By the time I had gotten there, the creatures outnumbered the king's army 2-1 because most of the villagers had not been able to flee behind the barricades. I gave them my message, and they brought in one captured creature which I showed the king how to dispatch. Even though they begged, I told them I had to leave in order to continue warning the rest of the west.

I spent the next two weeks riding from village to village warning those that were uninfected of what was coming, and helping them prepare defenses. I only came upon a corrupted village a quarter of the time that I went in. This made me think that I was riding ahead of the plague for the most part. It became difficult to find a safe place to stay because I was traveling alone, and did not have a partner to help keep watch on the road. I got into a couple o' scrapes with a few bandits and highwaymen, but generally they were no match for a knight.

I crossed the river Shannon planning on heading to their village on the way to Limerick, and those were my last stops before heading to Galway where I had heard rumors that the high king was massing his forces to take back an entirely overrun Dublin. It was not far from here that I, having ridden all day and being tired, had fallen asleep in the saddle. Normally, this would have been no problem as my horse will continue on the path without my encouragement, but perhaps being so near the river had messed up her sense hearing or of smell, and I awoke as she rode accidentally into the middle of a horde. Imagine my shock and surprise upon waking to be surrounded by the things.

The creatures had managed to close around us as the path had narrowed. My horse spooked and threw me, then bolted. She had knocked down a few as she fled, so I decided to run after her. I had mail on, but the rest of my armor was on the horse, but I had my sword. I cut through the beasts knowing how to easily dispatch them, but then I faced three together.

They had me distracted, so I didn't notice the fourth that had fallen in the grass as the horse passed. It took a chunk out of my leg before I noticed what happened. I stabbed down hard, but another grabbed my hand and caused me to jerk my sword back over my head in a weird fashion. Ended up putting that gash on my back there myself. Foolish. Anyway, it was not long after this that I broke through, limping, living off of pure battle energy, and went off after my horse. I fell, and saw my horse run up the path without me.

I was losing energy fast and decided to climb a tree to sleep. I had a bit of food on me, and knew that I would be in a sorry spot if I didn't rest. I slept for hours, waking only to the sounds of many moans passing underneath me. This continued for an hour before I finally fell asleep again. I woke up this morning wishing I had my horse once again. I continued on all day searching for her. I had assumed that she was lost forever, but around midafternoon, I found her tracks intersecting with two other horses, that then turned and headed away from me. I was on the right path, but I also saw the shuffling footprints of many of the creatures I had met before following them too.

Delirium kept me going. I had nothing else to do but follow the horde and hope they were leading me to my horse or to help. As the sun lost its power, I noticed the tracks split. The creatures had gone east on towards Shannon, but the horses had turned back west at the split on the trail. I took a chance assuming that I wouldn't be of much help to Shannon in my state, and followed the horses. I've been on your trail for hours. I saw the mark on the tree in the fading light, and thought that whoever I was following must have known what was going on. As I came into this area, it felt too quiet as if nature knew I was not alone. I headed towards the hill hoping that it would be a place that a well-trained warrior would know to hide. And, well, you know the rest I think."

We all sat flabbergasted at the story that Walter had just shared with us. The fact that he was still alive at all was a testament to his battle prowess and endurance as a great warrior. He had done his king and country a great service, and ours too. The effort that Sir Walter took to tell us his story was almost too much for him. He, with a serious effort, was having trouble keeping his eyes open. However, he demanded that we tell him what we had seen since we had parted ways.

We told him of our seemingly endless days in the saddle, Fernwood and the building of defenses, and finally the rescue of Molly which led ultimately to Shannon and our run in two days before with the cannibal tribe that had taken up residence there. We described their forest filled with the creatures, and how they had attempted to smash us in between the creatures and themselves.

We then told him how we had burned down their thatch, and discovered that we could turn the creatures against their masters. It was with a huge lump in my throat that I told him that we had discovered that injuring the cannibals had caused them to become prey, and the villagers covering themselves in mud which we assumed they did to mask their smell from the creatures. We then told him how we had split up at the fork in the road, and Sean and Edward shared how they came across his horse. Walter was smiling by the end of our story, but he seemed on the edge of ultimate collapse. He addressed us as we finished,

"Men, you have done really well for yourselves and represented your fathers loyally and courageously as knights. You have managed in the month since you became knights to have more adventure, save more lives, and do more damage on your enemies than most knights do in their entire life. I'm proud of you lads."

He then got a weird look on his face and said, "I'm not long for this world, my friends. You must continue up to Galway and meet up with the king there. You must finish your quest for your father, Banion, and continue to warn the people of what is coming, if they haven't already met with it themselves. You must give aid to any who ask of it, and you must save Ireland."

We tried to interrupt telling him that he wouldn't die, but he cut us off. "Don't. I have more experience with this plague than you boys do. Once bitten, there is no life but unlife. You must finish me after I die so that I do not come back as one of those things. Make me one more promise before I leave this place. " We promised that we would do whatever he asked of us. "After all this is over, and Ireland is back on the way to peace, you must go find my father in England and you must give him this badge and tell him my story."

Sir Walter reached inside his cloak and brought out a square piece of steel. Etched into the seal was the coat of arms of the Saxon family. Tell him, that I died with a sword in me hand, and a smile on me face." We all took the oath that Walter had asked of us. When we had promised, the look of pain upon his face changed to one of immense peace. Not long after, he gave up to the ghost, and we knelt and prayed for God to welcome his soul into heaven.

CHAPTER 25

We dug a grave for Sir Walter on the top of the hill. Edward gently slipped his knife into Walter's head making sure that he could not come back as a creature. We buried him as the sun began to rise in the east, and stacked stones upon the grave to mark that a great man had been buried there. Walter's longbow had snapped off of his horse's saddle, so we used it to fashion a cross for his grave. I took his extra arrows to augment my dwindling supply.

We looked through Walter's things as we ate breakfast, all of us wanting to leave this place in a hurry. We found a solid map of western Ireland that should help us get from where we were, up to Galway, and over to Dublin after that if we needed it to. It did not show the northern part of our country. Maybe Walter had intended to go back home after warning much of the country of the plague. We also found a rather stout dagger which Edward took and added to his belt, some armor that would not fit any of us but which we could sell, and three golden arm rings. These had not been used for hundreds of years since the Norse had ravaged Ireland's shores.

It was a bit odd that Walter had any, but we realized what he had them for when we saw our names engraved on them. Walter had planned on giving them to us as an ancient way of marking us men and as successful warriors.

We took them as a personal way to each remember Walter and all that he had done for us. We put our arm rings on underneath our leathers and felt as though we would always have that great warrior with us no matter what.

We packed up the horses, making the older one from Fernwood become our new pack horse. Edward took Walter's warhorse and we continued on as well as we could towards Galway. We were all rather quiet that morning and stopped only briefly to feed and water the horses, and eat a bit ourselves. As we mounted back up, I noticed a worried look on Sean's usually cheerful face. I addressed him, "Sean, mate, what's got you in a bind?"

He stared at me for a minute, and answered honestly "Banion, what of our fathers? What about Cork? If the plague has stretched out this far into Ireland already, and has already taken over whole villages, then how can we know that our families are still safe? If the plague arrives in Cork, there could be thousands of them things there already. Your uncle's left Dublin after all. The ancient seat of our kings for centuries. If Dublin can be taken over and your uncle's great knights pushed back, what about our family?"

He was right of course. We hadn't even spoken much of Cork since we had left. This was mostly because of the overwhelming urgency of our situation and our desire to finish our quest with honor. We had met so many new people, helped so many, that we had almost forgotten our own. Edward stopped his horse looking alarmed and we three gathered together to think of what to do next. I saw

Fang glance our way after we had stopped, and then head off into the woods. He probably saw this as a great time to look for some fresh game for his dinner. We decided to make camp even though it was still afternoon.

We sat, that evening under the stars and next to the fire and weighed our options. The discussion really came down to whether we should turn back and find our way back home to help our families, or to continue on our mission that our fathers had put before us. It was a choice between family and honor. An impossible choice. We knew that we had no idea what we might find weeks from now when we made it back to Cork; if we made it back. We also knew that between here and there could be miles and miles filled with creatures. We were not far from where my uncle was to be. If we continued on we would fulfill not only our own mission, but the mission of Sir Walter who had not faltered in his duty even far away from his father's love until his very last breath.

Our arguments went on late into the night. We all argued for and against continuing on, and for and against going back. In the end, we had come so far for our fathers' sakes that we could not cast aside our quest so easily. Plus, my uncle might have need of us. Ireland might have need of us, and we did not want to let her down. This was our duty. This was our pledge. We resigned ourselves to the fact that, whatever the danger, we could not give up on what we were meant to do. So we would head north now. To Galway and to the king.

CHAPTER 26

Fang came back in the early morning as I was on watch. He had blood around his mouth, and feathers in his fur. He had an almost haughty attitude as he flopped down next to me, successful with his hunt. "Watch that pride," I laughed at him and scratched his ears. He began to clean himself as I stoked the fire and started our breakfast.

We were back on the trail an hour later. We had, for the most part, gotten used to life on the trail. We, although miserable, had stopped complaining about being up at dawn for another day in the saddle. I think we all knew that something must happen soon because the area we were headed into was much more densely populated than the parts of the west we had previously been in.

I checked Walter's map at noon as we crossed an open field. I felt slightly exposed and felt as if we were being watched. We should soon have been coming to a river crossing that would take us into the county below Galway. We would be there in another week if we didn't get slowed up too much. It was another hour before the river became loud enough to hear. The sounds of the animals in the woods brought a feeling of comfort to us which we had not felt for days. Sean was about to set off to scout the road ahead when I called to him to look out for a stone bridge that crossed the river. He waved a hand as he went up the road, and I was glad to see Fang tear off after him. None of us liked going anywhere alone anymore.

Sean came back about half an hour later saying that he had found the bridge but there was a bit of a problem. The bridge had a guard, and that guard was a fully armored knight. There was also a rich pavilion on the other side of the bridge where we could assume this knight took his rest. As we approached, I saw many bodies of his victims floating down by the bank where he had unceremoniously dropped them after killing them. There was also a ring of dead creatures around our side of the bridge, marking out a twenty foot semi-circle around the bridge. This was not a man to take lightly.

"Fang, heel," I called as Sean and Edward drew their weapons, one on either side of me. I had my bow across my lap with an arrow already on the string. The arrow had a bodkin point on it instead of the usual broad head. A broad head would do more damage and would kill something like a man or a deer quickly, but this man had armor on. The bodkin's slim and pointed design was made to be used to try to pierce mail and armor. Even if it didn't, however, the force of an arrow at the range we were entering would likely knock the knight back if not flat on his back. Thus, I could keep him distracted and slowed and Sean or Edward could disarm him.

The knight stood calmly on the bridge as we came towards him. He had an unsheathed sword in his hand with its tip resting calmly on the ground next to him. He seemed unmoved at the arrival of three other knights. Perhaps it was because we were not fully armored that he did not see us as a threat, or perhaps it was because he wanted to see what we would do. He stepped towards us when we had stopped inside the ring of dead bodies next to his bridge. He came to the edge of the bridge and Fang let out a low growl as a warning. Next the knight spoke, "Hail, fellow knights of Ireland. I can tell by how you carry yourselves and what you wear that you are nobly born. I hate to tell such esteemed guests bad news, but this road into Kiltartan is closed. You will have to find another way."

Sean sneered at the man and responded before we could take full measure of this man. "And what are you going to do to stop all three of us and the wolf?"

At his words the knight of the bridge began to laugh. He responded to Sean with such confidence that it should have given us warning. "What," he cried, "three baby knights and a dog? Whatever will I do with such as you wee lads." At this, he swung his sword up in front of himself with such speed that it did not even register that he had moved. He swung it around his head in a complicated pattern of moves that mesmerized all three of us. Sean had just talked back to an expert swordsman without giving us much chance to try to talk our way past. It seemed then that the only way we would now get across that bridge was if we fought our way across.

The knight continued as his sword once again came to rest by his side. "But you are right little knight, it is not fair to have three against one is it?" Sean bridled at being called little, but held his tongue this time. "Perhaps," continued the knight "we should even the odds." He called out loudly over his shoulder. "Brother! Come join me and help me hold the bridge of our father's fathers."

At this, a second knight as broad of shoulder as the first came out of the pavilion similarly prepared for battle except he carried a massive war axe on his shoulder. I could see Sean's face burning red with embarrassment at the mess he had gotten us in to, but it was not too late, I thought naively. I addressed the two knights as the second joined the first. "Brave knights, we are not your enemies. The only enemy to Ireland is the plague that I can see you have already come across guarding your bridge. However, it saddens me to see that you have dispatched men as well. Why, I ask in the name of the king, have you killed your countrymen in this place."

"In the name of the king, you say?" Chided the second knight. "And who might you be to speak with such authority? Not the king we think. Ireland has no king anymore. Ireland is no more." I shook with anger at his words. "You disloyal pigs!" I cried. "How can you so quickly forget your vows when Ireland needs you most? Stand down and surrender your arms in arrest and be brought to trial for treason. I am Banion, prince of Cork, knight of the realm. Kneel!"

The authority in my voice surprised me as much as it did the knights on the bridge. They looked at one another, neither speaking as if in disbelief. "We did not think the kingdom continued on," said the first knight. "All the rumors tell that the kingdom has fallen and that we must all fend for ourselves. We are keeping our lands free from any that bring the plague. None can be trusted."

The second knight continued after, "We shall tell our sons of your bravery Banion, but now you must die." The words had not even left his mouth when he and his brother started for us. There were twenty feet in front of us giving us seconds to prepare. I drew my bow back to its full length and loosed the arrow at the second bridge knight's chest as he approached Sean to my right. The arrow hit him in the right side piercing his armor, and snapping a rib. It checked his pace for a moment as he howled in rage. This gave Sean enough time to kick free of his horse, and swing his hammer with full strength at the knight's other side. The knight parried at the last second with his war axe, and the two of them fought chest to chest, strength to strength.

I dropped my bow, dismounting as the first crossbow bolt hit the ground near my feet. Across the bridge was who must have been the knight's squire who frantically spun the crank to ready another arrow. I drew Oíche and called to Fang as I headed towards the first knight as he hammered his sword into Edward's shield. "Fang," I yelled "enemy." I pointed across the bridge and Fang took off.

I caught the first knight's sword with mine as he tried to shatter Edward's shield. This gave a kneeling Edward time to regain his balance, and we attacked the first knight together. He was bigger and faster than the both of us and kept his balance with a practiced step as he parried our blows and pressed his own attack. Another bolt hit near my right flank and I was lucky the crossbowman had missed. It was dangerous to be firing at a target so close to his ally, but it did not seem to stop him. I heard a scream and a flash of gray and black out of the corner of my eye as Fang reached the archer and removed that threat.

The scream caused the first knight to turn almost imperceptibly towards his pavilion, and Edward and I pushed our attack. We could hear grunting behind us and the definite crack and chime of the axe and hammer connecting nearby. The first knight, to regain his position, took a wild flat swing across our chests in order to make us leap back, but it was flimsy, and we took our advantage when it was given to us. Edward stepped in behind the knight's swing and shield checked him hard, popping the knight's shoulder out of place. I brought Oíche down hard on the wrist holding his sword and cut through bone and tendon, severing the hand from the arm.

The knight's scream was cut short as Edward's axe fell sharply into the groove between gorget and helm. Almost entirely removing the knight's head. As his body fell, we turned towards Sean in time to see the second knight parry and try to slam the haft of his axe down on Sean's right arm. Sean stepped forward and headbutted the knight in the face, breaking his nose, the only exposed portion of his face and head. Sean then twisted to his left, spun on his pivot foot and brought his hammer up into the knight's stomach. There was an explosion of breath out of the knight as he doubled over, and Sean finished him with an overhand chop that crushed the back of his neck.

Sean himself fell to his knees in exhaustion seconds

afterward. We had won a spectacular victory, but all felt the shame of the fact that we were fighting against men in these troubled times. Fang came back licking his bloody chops in a gruesome display. We caught the horses and crossed the bridge to the pavilion. There we found water and food and bedrolls already arranged.

It was hardly afternoon, but we knew we would be staying here tonight. We used the wood from the bridge to burn the bodies that afternoon and we fashioned a cross to plant near where the bridge had stood. This place had cost many men their lives, and those men would have been needed in the coming battle to take Ireland back from the undead. We fell heavily onto the prepared bedrolls exhausted before the sun had even set. Fang, hardly tired, lay at the edge of the tent and watched up the path towards our future. He kept watch for whatever danger would come next.

CHAPTER 27

The next morning the three of us woke in surprise. We had all slept the whole night through without a guard and without a thought of the consequences. Fang sat by the door still guarding and had not woken any of us during the night to take our turns. It was with huge gratitude that we gave Fang a huge hunk of dried venison to eat for breakfast and he scarfed it down before curling up in the blankets I had just disentangled myself from.

We dragged a table from inside the pavilion outside and sat it in the sun. We sat and enjoyed the simplicity of the river as it passed by not knowing of the chaos ripping through the country that it swam through. We pulled out Walter's map and thought about how far we had come and how close we were to getting some much needed answers.

We spent the morning cleaning our weapons and armor from the fight the day before, knowing that we should have done this the previous day. However, we could not do it with the poor, bloated bodies of the bridge knights' victims lying so close.

Edward left after lunch with Fang to scout the road ahead and see how safe the area we were in was. Fang had slept in the pavilion since the early morning and was then restless and wanted to run. What an amazing beast he was.

Fang had saved our lives a countless amount of times so far on this quest, and I think that all three of us noticed how lucky we were to have him with us. We could have easily woken up with a knife to our throats or a creature biting into our bodies, but had stayed safe through the whole night.

Sean and I checked through the pavilion for supplies and were not able to find much. We think that it was most likely that the two bridge knights and their squire had been living off the river. A thought that turned disgusting as we thought of the ten rotting bodies we had pulled out of it the previous afternoon. Their bedrolls were good, and we were able to find one horse tied in a small paddock nearby.

There were trappings enough for three horses, but we assumed that either the squire had set them free, or his screams and the snarls of Fang had caused them to run. The one that was left was a beauty though. A dark black warhorse that had obviously been taken well care of. This would allow us to use Sean's old warhorse, the one that Sir Stephan had given us in Fernwood, as another pack animal which would mean that for the first time in almost a month, the three of us would be well horsed on a breed meant for battle.

Edward came back without much to report. The afternoon was dwindling, and he could tell us nothing other than it seemed that there must be a village not far away because the land was planted close by. We decided to spend one more night in the pavilion and to continue on our journey the following morning. We posted a guard that night rather than risking fate once again. The night passed by without incident and we woke the following morning more refreshed than we had in the weeks since we left Fernwood and its beds.

We began to pack up the horses and what little supplies we found in the pavilion. We decided to leave the pavilion standing where it was. It was too big for us to carry around with us, and really could do nothing more than be a burden to the horses. It is not like we saw ourselves having the time or energy to put it up. So maybe it would be a haven to more weary travelers in the future. This would allow it to regain honor after the dishonor shown by its previous inhabitants.

We were nearly ready to depart as morning light crept into the sky when Fang began to bark hysterically over towards the river. The sounds that he was making were odd. They weren't a warning, but they were not the sound he would make for one of us returning. It was somewhere in between. Confused, as if Fang did not know what he was seeing. I drew Oíche as we ran towards the barks, hushing Fang as we ran up. The sight that met our eyes is something that will haunt my dreams for the rest of my life.

There, standing completely still in the mud on the other side of the river was a girl. She had become stuck in the mud apparently after trying to walk directly into the river, and she was not alone. Behind her were four other children. Three boys and another girl. I fell to my knees beside Fang and Sean and Edward did the same as we all understood the bewildered sound of Fang's barks. He had seen children, but could smell the creatures that they were. All of the five children had turned. There was no indication as to where they had come from, and there was nothing we could do as the others made it to the edge of the river and also sunk past their knees in the mud. A choked sound came from me and, as the sound reached across the river, the five children raised their hands longingly out to us and issued a tired moan of hunger.

Fang trembled beside me, and, after an eternity, I was able to turn my eyes away from them and back to my companions. Edward had tears in his eyes, and Sean had his head bowed as he prayed. We did not know what else to do, knowing that we could not end them, and so we prayed together, went back to the horses, mounted, and rode away.

CHAPTER 28

The sight of the children pushed us all into a depression. We rode in silence for hours stopping only briefly to rest the horses and eat a small meal. We continued on into the afternoon without seeing anyone or anything. Edward had been right; the area did seem inhabited, but we could not find life to go along with the signs we were seeing.

Our path eventually took us to an abandoned farmhouse. The door was broken off its hinges, and there were many footprints around the door and the windows. This seemed to imply activity of the undead, as we had started calling them, knowing now how the plague kept them moving after their deaths. The Holy Word spoke of the dead rising and walking once again among the living, but none of us could remember what it said after that, or what any of it meant.

We spent two more days passing abandoned homes and shelters, finding one farm completely engulfed in flames as we rode up. Still, we found no one alive or any dead for that matter. The world seemed to have abandoned itself. We were running dangerously low on food. We could find water easily enough, but had already been rationing our food for days. Even Fang would return without success from his hunts and he would be gone for hours assumedly having to venture farther and farther without any luck.

When our hope seemed to be at rock bottom, chance gave us a path to take. We couldn't have been but a handful of days from Galway and so we hoped to see some sign of the king, and then finally it happened.

We exited the woods as our path began to cut into a wide field. We could see some of the large fairy stones of the old people in the middle of the field. As we began to make our way towards them, we saw a single rider break away from the shadows beneath them and tear off away from us towards the opposing tree line. We broke into a gallop trying to catch the one person we had seen since the bridge knights, but by the time we made it to the stones, he was long gone.

We knew the direction he had taken, and even found a small campsite there near the stones. We wondered if he had been a forward scout whose job was to watch the road from the south to see if any more knights would come. If this was the case, we were probably not more than a day or two away from the king's forces.

As we contemplated this and began to search our surroundings we finally discovered a clue as to what direction to travel. Sir Walter and the messenger had not known where in Galway the king was, but finally, off to the east, we saw the smoke from more than one fire. It was all we needed, and we hastily remounted and headed in that direction.

Our spirits were revived at the thought of human companionship, but our experience in Shannon and at the bridge had made us wary. Of course, this new wariness of anyone we did not know could also explain why the rider had taken off rather than see who we were. We outnumbered him, and it would not have been worth it to risk his life just for a name. All this aside, we had hope again. We rode towards the smoke and the tree line with our eyes open, but with smiles on our faces.

We rode for two hours in search of the fire or the rider and found nothing. We knew we must be getting close because we were starting to smell the smoke from the fires. The sound of moaning followed by many piercing screams told us that we had found people, but not how we had hoped to be reunited with the living.

We rode around the next bend to find that the path evened out and headed towards a small village in what would have been a quite beautiful meadow. Half the town, unfortunately, was on fire, and it seemed like half the town was also trying to eat the other half.

We could see that a few figures had climbed the thatch of the blacksmith's shop, while others had boarded up their doors. We rode towards the village center and saw many of the undead pounding on doors, reaching for the impossible victims on the roof, or feasting on their fellow villagers on the ground.

A couple of men were bashing at the creatures with pitchforks and hoes, but they were hitting them in the arms, legs, and torsos and the creatures just continued to stand up and attack. We passed the blacksmith who had a hammer in each hand as he tried to tear through ranks of the undead to get to the front door of the great hall. He yelled in triumph as we rode past and I took the head off of one creature with Oíche as we passed. Sean jumped down from his horse and went to help the blacksmith. We had left our other two horses tied on the outskirts of the village knowing they would just get in our way.

"Zip! Zip," went Edward's sling and the creatures rushing towards us fell back with crushed skulls. I barreled into a group of the beasts on my huge horse and, being trained in battle, my horse, began to kick out with his front and back feet as I cut down viciously with my blade. We broke away from the group about the time the unthinking monsters realized that we were there. I jumped down and smacked the back of my horse so it would go back to the others, and I met Edward as he did the same.

Sean and the blacksmith were hammering away into the horde at the door, and I heard Sean yell for him to "Smash 'em in the 'ead!" Edward and I covered their backs knowing they were exposed as they focused on the monsters in front of them. Edward and I covered each other's flanks and made short work of the creatures that ran towards us thinking we were easy prey. We saw some of the men fall as they tried to protect their families, and could do nothing. We were splintering the undead, and would soon have most of them down. As the people watched, a few of the men saw how we fought, and with courage, jumped down from their roofs and began to fight alongside us.

It was nearly an hour later when Sean stopped and leaned against his hammer in the yard. We were given almost a second to relax before another scream sounded inside a nearby cottage. Edward kicked in the door and led with his shield before him, and Sean and I followed. Inside, backed against a grubby table was girl near our age with beautiful red hair. What must have been her mother and little brother, turned, were trying to get to her with gaping mouths. She pushed them back with a stool, and continued to scream.

Edward pushed the little boy hard with his shield, and knocked him back through the back door and out into the street. The girl, in a fear driven rage, took the chance when only facing one of them, and cracked the stool over the woman's head. She went down, and I made sure that she did not rise again.

Edward reentered from out back as we led the girl out the front door to where the rest of the survivors had gathered. She fell into the arms of a short, older woman and they both sank down to the ground in tears. We crossed ourselves as we finally were able to breathe, and at once the townsfolk surrounded us.

They let out a great many cheers at our timely rescue. We were taken into the great hall, and given as much food as we could eat as a few of the men began to clear the village and make sure we had gotten them all. A couple of the village elders, who had hidden in the hall in the beginning of the attack sat down with us, and most of the rest of the village began dragging bodies to the center of the village square amidst the cries and wails of those who had begun to mourn their losses.

The elders told us how a stranger had shown up the night before on a horse and seemed to be sick. One of the widows had taken him in to help bring him back to health. He, we figured out, must have turned during the night and bitten her, and then the two of them began attacking their neighbors. The morning had erupted into chaos, and had continued until our arrival. We told them who we were and our quest, and, upon hearing our names, they practically fell out of their seats out of fear. They had never imagined sitting at the table with the son of a king and two more nobly born knights.

The truth of the matter was that at this point we looked nothing close to nobly born. Our clothes were torn and tattered. From head to toe, we were covered in the dust of the road, and mud and blood had stained us in ways that would not wash off easily.

The old men confirmed the rumors that the king was not far away. They had not seen him, but there had been messengers pass through on their way south and east. The king was demanding that all true born knights and men at arms of Ireland meet in the fields of Athenry in county Galway. He intended to march on Dublin and, after retaking the city, make it a defensible safe haven where the survivors of Ireland could regroup with port access to the rest of the world.

The rumors from some sailors that had made it back here after landing in Galway a few weeks before were that the plague had spread across all of Europe. They had no idea that it had already come to Ireland, and we shared what we had found out of the ship coming to the south and spreading the plague inland toward Killarney.

That evening all of the survivors of the village came in to the great hall and gathered there eating and waiting to see what would happen next. The rumors of who we were spread quickly around and we were asked for our advice on what they should be doing next. Half of the village had burned, and over half of the villagers were dead. We gave them two options.

The first choice was that they could make their town as defensible as they could, and then try to defend themselves as best they could. We promised to stay for a couple of days and oversee their defensive strategy, but these were farmers, and the wives of farmers. All but the blacksmith seemed like sheep without a shepherd.

Their other option was to put what little valuables they had on their backs, and seek out shelter in Galway. That was the biggest city center in this part of the country, but we also did not know if it had been overrun or not either. They, if they took that option, could literally be walking directly towards their own gruesome deaths. They didn't really have much of an option though. Edward walked the village with one of the men while this conversation took place, and gave me a negative sign when he walked back in. The village would be too hard to defend if a horde made its way here.

The people did not want to leave. Many of them had never been outside of the village boundaries before let alone the county boundaries. Only the blacksmith, an elder, and two men who had been sailors had ever been to Galway itself. The villagers argued for hours.

The blacksmith, a man named O'Malley, was the leader of the side arguing to leave. The older people of the village were afraid, and rightly so. There was no promise that this group with its women, children, and elders would even survive the walk, but there were probably fifteen to twenty men who could protect the group now they knew how to fight and put down the creatures.

I had started to drift off in my exhaustion of the day when the girl we had rescued walked in. She still had tears in her eyes as she looked at the three of us, and then the rest of the village. "You fools!" She began, "there is nothing left for us here. Our families are dead. Not one of us has escaped loss. Only half of the village still stands. What are we to live here for? We must fight. We must join up with any left in Galway, and we must fight for our land."

Her words were passionate, and their effect seemed to be instantaneous. A few people tried to argue against her, but were quickly shouted down by the others who recognized the truth to her words. Her name was Reilly, and she was beautiful.

The town posted guards that night, and all there began to pack. We fetched our horses and gladly gave over their care to a few boys from the village. The next morning, at dawn, the village was ready to move. We would lead them for most of the day before turning farther to the north to continue on to Athenry. They would then have to go on for two more days of walking to Galway on their own. They were not happy about this, but it was very hard for them to have the courage to stand up to a knight. Let alone, a knight prince.

O'Malley had taken over as the leader of the group, and talked up in the front of the column with Edward for much of the day. Edward later told me that he had once been a warrior before receiving a leg injury that caused him to put down his blades and begin making more for others. I saw the girl, Reilly, riding not far ahead of Sean and me. I caught her many times looking in my direction, only to look away suddenly as if she were focusing on something else when I turned her way.

CHAPTER 29

Two mishaps happened over the next twenty four hours as we escorted the villagers towards Galway. The first happened mere hours after we left the village. A few of the older villagers had fallen back to the rear of the group and were slowing with the difficulty of the pace. Sean rode as the rearguard with two of the village men, but they were about fifteen minutes behind the main force of the village. The scene they came upon and later recounted was one of horror.

They found the packs of three of the older men lying on the blood covered ground. A woman's hair sash was found fluttering off the path on the unmistakable blood trail of multiple dragged away bodies. We could only assume that four of the old ones had stopped to rest and had been taken by creatures hiding in the nearby field. No one heard their screams as they had fallen back far enough from the main host, and Sean and his men had not caught up to them yet. This event gave an unmistakable mood of dread and fear over the whole group, and had mothers screaming at the call of any bird, or the breaking of any twig.

We almost had an uprising on our hands when a couple of villagers sat down in the path and refused to move another inch until the army came and got them. When a loudmouthed teen shouted that they would be the next victims of the creatures hiding in the field, the villagers, realizing their situation, got up and continued on the path set before them.

We knew that the villagers had been put in between a rock and a hard place. Edward and I could not help but feel sorry for them. They were handling the fact that they had just been attacked by their neighbors and forced to flee their homes really well. There were hardly any complaints as these people realized that the world had changed. This was the spirit or Ireland. We, as a people, when affected by diversity, will overcome and continue on steadfast into our futures.

The second mishap happened during the middle of the night. We had stopped in the forest to make camp, posted sentries, and collapsed, as a group, into exhaustion. Sean, Edward, and I all took different watches so that there would always be one of us in charge. We would make our rounds of the sentries and make sure that all was well. It was then, in the deepest and darkest part of the night, that we were all woken up by the screams of a man on the far side of camp.

We rushed towards the sound, weapons drawn with torches in our hands. Edward was there first because he was on guard at the time, and he found two of the creatures feasting on one of the sentries. He had apparently fallen asleep at his post, and had only woken as the creatures began to eat his legs. It was a grisly scene.

Most of the villagers ran up and made a circle around

the man who was still alive after Edward had arrived and had dispatched the creatures. The man was in enormous pain and feared death so he didn't do much other than scare the rest of the villagers and make them assume that their own deaths were nigh.

No one slept for the rest of that night, and there were mutterings of going back to the village as we got ready to leave. The eventual realization that there was nothing to go back to was enough to get the villagers moving again as the sun began to rise. We had been on the move for a little over a day, and had had two miserable experiences losing people. The group morale was low, and it did not seem to have a chance to get better as the rain began to fall. Now, no one wanted to continue, we were losing people, and it was miserably wet and cold. The blacksmith rescued the group as he began to sing aloud a song of work and fortitude. His high and happy voice carried throughout the entire group and people began to smile as he refused to give up on their struggle.

By early afternoon the rain had stopped. We reached the fork in the road that lead to either Galway or Athenry, and knew this meant that we would have to leave the villagers behind. Some begged us to stay with them, some demanded that it was our duty to protect them, and others continued walking as if they did not have a hope in the world.

Reilly was really not happy. She asked if she could accompany us to the king to help fight this plague. We refused her on the grounds that she was not a soldier, and that her fellow villagers needed her more than anything. She huffed and rode down the other path not looking back. It was painful to have her react this way. I wanted her to be safe, and I felt that not heading into more immediate danger was one way to make sure she was.

Edward, Sean, and I rode on. We prayed for the villagers before leaving them, and then left knowing that we had a duty to get to the king as quickly as possible. There were indications that others had ridden the path we were on recently, and that encouraged us to continue on with more pressing speed.

It was the middle of the afternoon when we realized we were being followed. Fang kept turning around and peering into the woods behind us and emitting a low growl. We continued on and occasionally one of us would stop and watch as the others continued to scout ahead. We now had one eye pointed forward to our goal, and one behind us wondering who was trying to keep up but remain out of sight.

We knew that come dark we would be in a vulnerable position. So, we decided to lay in ambush that evening and see who had been dogging our steps. We left Fang off of the road about a hundred yards down the path. Edward then took the horses farther up the path as if we had continued going. Sean and I took up positions on either side of the path where we were able to conceal ourselves. After about thirty minutes, Fang came running back to us and crouched down beside me. Whoever it was must have been approaching.

Slowly a figure emerged in the half light. After they passed by us, we sprang our trap. We burst forth from the hedges and closed in on the lone rider swiftly. Sean grabbed them and pulled them out of the saddle. The person yelped with surprise and struggled mightily at being caught. It wasn't until their hood fell back that we realized it was a woman who had been following us. It was not just any woman either, but Reilly.

She cursed at us and Sean laughed when he realized who it was and pulled her up to her feet. She seemed upset that she had been caught, and so we didn't make it easy for her.

"Well," I said. "You are lucky that you were caught by friends rather than enemies out here in the wild. There is no telling what would have happened to you had you come across bandits or worse. Your fellow villagers would never even know that you disappeared. You just suddenly would be gone forever"

Sean continued where I left off, "yes, you might have become naught more than a blood trail. And even then, that is only if there was someone to come after and look for ye."

At this point, Edward had ridden back to us and looked amused as he noticed who had been following us. "Ms. Reilly," He said. "Seems you took a wrong turn and ended up on the road to Athenry instead of Galway. Surely you did not refuse the command of your prince when he told you to continue on with the rest of your village? A crime such as that is punishable by law. So it is."

If we thought we had her scared at all, then we were much mistaken. Reilly glared at us defiantly and responded in a quite reasonable way actually. "It is not up to you three boys to decide my fate," said Reilly. "I can come and go as I please and you cannot stop me. If it is my desire to go to Athenry, then I will. Who are you to try to stop a free woman from traveling the roads?"

The three of us burst into laughter as she said this. It was comical how she called us boys but described herself as a free woman. We three being at least two years older than she. She scoffed at us, and I asked the only logical next question. "What are you doing here, Reilly? Seriously, this is dangerous to come running off by yourself. What if you had been surrounded by the creatures out here by yourself?"

Her response was not what I had been expecting. She suddenly burst into tears and stood there sobbing next to her horse. We looked at one another wishing that one of us knew what to do next. She began to try to choke through some words after a few minutes. "I have nothing left. Me mum was killed in the attack, as was my little brother. What am I supposed to do? I have nothing left except neighbors, and they would have me married to one of them to become someone's wife who I cared nothing for. They would expect me to just take up the mantle of cook and cleaner and be a mother. How can I bring children into a world like this? No. No, I will fight back in any way that I can. I cannot rest until Ireland is at peace again. Only then will I know that my family is resting."

We could not argue with her reasoning. We would not want our lives dictated to us the way she just described. I reached into my saddle bags and pulled out Sir Walter's Seax. The Seax was a stout short sword. It was much shorter than a sword and used as a backup weapon for many English warriors where Walter was from. For Reilly though, it could be wielded like a full sized sword. "Might as well be ready for them when they come," I said. She looked at the knife and then nodded to each of us in turn appreciatively. She wiped her eyes and put the knife on her belt. Nothing else needed to be said at this point. We all mounted and rode on for another hour before finding a likely spot to camp for the night. Suddenly, we three were four.

CHAPTER 30

The next morning we were up and off by dawn. We would be reaching the king hopefully by the afternoon. As we got closer to Athenry, the signs of a well-traveled road became apparent. Many smaller paths and roads joined the one we were on as it broadened. This path was a popular one to Galway and it was clear that many men and horses had come this way not too long before.

We ate a boring lunch and continued on. The three of us and Fang were quite tired of dried meat at this point in our travels, but could not complain since we still had something to eat. We had come to be very low on our food stores when we reached Reilly's village. Luckily for us, the villagers had refilled our bags seeing as they could not carry all that was in the village on their own backs.

It wasn't long after getting into this region that we met our first rider. A messenger came tearing towards us on his way towards Galway. We hailed him and he slowed down. We could tell that he did not mean to stop and speak to us because what he saw were four much disheveled travelers and what to him must have been one mean looking dog.

Knowing his reluctance to be stopped on his delivery, Edward called out "Stop in the name of Sir Banion, prince of Cork." The effect was immediate. I did not really like to use my status much. In fact, I much rather preferred to seem equal to my friends as a knight. However, it was quite effective at times to mention who I was.

The messenger almost flipped over his horse's head as he pulled the reins hard. He bowed to me, noticing then that we were not mere travelers but knights of the realm. I addressed him, "Do you come from the king? Where do you go, and what is your message?"

He replied, "Begging your pardon, my prince. I did not recognize you for who you were as I hurried on my way. My name is Orin, Sir Knights. I do come from the king. He gathers a host at Athenry, but he has not gotten as many as he expected. It seems the war is being hard fought all over the country, and it is hard for his lords to come this way. He has sent me to Galway to hire boat and send for aid among all the regions of Ireland. We lost nearly half our men when Dublin turned against us."

"What war?" Sean gaped. "What is the state of this country? Has it gotten worse than even we could imagine?"

Edward sat with a worried look on his face but did not add anything. The messenger continued, "Brave knight, it does not go well for us. It has been little more than a fortnight since we fled Dublin. We had no chance there. We did not understand what we were up against. The king, at first, intended to fortify the castle and prepare for the siege. However, after closing the doors, we realized that some who had been bitten were inside, not yet turned as it were. Their screams pierced the night, and by dawn the king and any who could ride were leaving the city in much haste.

Reports indicate that the plague has traveled almost over the whole country at this point. All this in a matter of weeks. Belfast has fallen, along with Dublin of course, Cork was holding its own, but we haven't heard from them in a week, and Galway is the only city currently whole and defensible. Word was able to get to them in time for them to prepare."

This news was worrying, and the lack of contact from Cork was enough to make all of us uneasy. The messenger took off not long after that to continue with his message towards the south. He told us that the king was not more than two hours ride from where we were right then. So, we continued on not knowing what was really ahead of us.

Another hour up the road and we were no longer the only men in the area or on the road. A sentry stopped us, and, after realizing who we were, took off ahead of us to announce our imminent arrival. It was good that the king would know we were coming before we got there. We were joined on the road by several different groups of knights. Some coming from the north and some from the middle of the country. There were none from the south, so we did not hear any new news about the fate of our home.

We came around a bend in the path, and there was the king's host displayed in all its glory on the field before us. There were hundreds of tents arrayed below, and we were met by a steward of the king who took us directly towards the king's tent. We said our goodbyes to the men we had ridden in with and laughed at their surprised faces when they realized who we were. Even Sean and Edwards' fathers were well known all over the country, and this caused not a little amount of pointing and hurried whispers as we passed.

We were taken to the king's personal stable where two boys came and took our horses. Reilly would not be able to accompany us into the king's presence. Therefore, she elected to stay with the horses and watch our stuff. Another steward led her away with the promise of a bath, food, and rest and she went without complaint. Sean, Edward, and I looked at each other and realized how bad we all looked. We tried to knock some of the mud off of our boots, and tried to straighten our hair and clothes, but it was no use. We were dusting off each other's backs when a booming voice told us to stop "acting like little girls."

My uncle, the high king of Ireland, walked out of his tent with a loud laugh. "Banion! Look at ye lad. You've right turned into a man haven't ye? I haven't seen you in too long me boy." He pulled me into a great bear hug and lifted me off the ground. He still towered over me even though I was by no means a small man. He towered over Sean too so I couldn't feel too bad. He shook hands with Sean and Edward and began to regale us with stories of all three of our fathers.

We went into the tent and found quite the practical military commander's tent. He might have been a king, but my uncle did not care much for wealth. There was a large wooden table with chairs around it, and then a pile of furs next to a big brazier of fire. He had two wolfhounds in the tent, and they quickly took to Fang after the king had grabbed Fang and began petting him behind the ears.

"Fang, you ole mangy mutt. I haven't seen you since Banion's dad and I found you when you were not more than a pup." Fang must have recognized his scent because he did not seem bothered at all by this large stranger treating him like a fuzzy bear. He rolled over on his back and let the king give him a good petting before the wolfhounds sheepishly made their way over to smell him. It wasn't long before they were helping Fang wash off the dirt of the road.

About this time, servants came in with enough food for a feast and the three of us dived in after assuring that Reilly had been given plenty as well. The king talked while we ate, and at first this was nothing more than him remembering old times or the battles he fought with our fathers by his side. The tide of the conversation turned abruptly as he talked of his only defeat. The recent loss of Dublin to the undead.

The king recounted the story that the messenger had told us but with greater detail. He shared, after we commended his messenger on a job well done, what their reactions had been as the plague started to take over. He had had news from my father of the plague and the new threat just as my father had learned them from Sir Walter. The king knew what to expect, but when it happened no one knew what to do. They hadn't expected it to be on their doorsteps mere days after hearing that something strange was coming across Europe. He hadn't expected to deal with any sickness at all until the next spring when the trading season had picked back up, but the creatures had come without mercy.

They would have been able to push back the creatures, but the city panicked. As one section of town fell to the sickness, others emptied as people tried to reach the safety of other places. All they really did was form big crowds, which attracted the creatures, which spread the infection even faster. Before Dublin knew what hit her, they had lost three quarters of the population. This was mostly the poor who did not have the means to defend themselves or hide in less populated areas.

My uncle had ridden out with a hundred knights in order to protect his fleeing citizens, but they turned on them and started attacking the knights to try to take their horses. He ended up having to retreat back to the castle and had lost several good knights. The creatures could now be seen from the castle battlements in the city below. They soon realized their lack of prey and turned towards the castle within a day as the last bit of the city holding out against their insatiable appetites.

The king had to make a decision. Knowing the port was lost, and having way too many people in the castle for him to support, he had left a small contingent of men at arms to protect the castle and the women and children, and he and all of his men had ridden away so that they would be able to fight on. They had charged through the hordes of the undead and beaten them back as they slashed and smashed their way through the city. He had lost men, but had finally broken free and headed west hoping to regroup in Galway. Ever since then, he had been here. Marshalling his forces and waiting for the chance to strike back against this plague and reclaim his country.

We later told the king our whole story from the trials through our most recent experience with the besieged village and their consequent flight towards Galway. He gasped several times during the telling of our story, and seemed outraged at some of the experiences we had. He, after we had finished our tale, let out a huge breath and said "Christ above, how you three have managed such hell is beyond me thinking." He turned at this and called a servant to him. He said, "I did not know that my nephew had another companion. Please go get her and bring her here."

Reilly was brought in a few minutes later looking scared and worried. The king assured her that she had his protection and was in safety. She realized, after sitting down with us, that she was amongst friends. At the same time, it was a bit unusual for a king to call a commoner into his presence let alone allow her to sit and eat with him. He explained that any companion of his nephew was one that he was willing to have near him which made me feel good and quite lucky to have such a generous king.

Finally, I had to ask the question that I had known was on our minds. "Uncle," I said. "What of Cork? All we have heard is that they were well defending last you heard from them, but that that had been almost a week." A dark look came over the king's face, and I could tell that he was worried about his brother, my father, as well. He looked at me with pity in his eyes, and was quiet for a few minutes before speaking.

"Lads, I wish I had any news at all to give ye. Last we heard, your father, Banion, and your fathers, Sean and Edward, were leading a stout defense of the south from Cork. They being the first that had heard of the plague, as evidenced by your trials, were able to prepare their defenses, call their soldiers, and get the commoners within the town walls of Cork. I know they had been attacked probably a week after you boys left.

It seems as if a whole village from north of the city had been turned, and had come south to Cork. The fighting was rough, but, with the knowledge that Sir Walter had shared, they were able to beat back the undead without much issue. Only a few commoners were bitten as they did not have mail on, and those were willing to be separated from the rest of the population knowing their fate.

That was a month ago, and yer father had sent a messenger twice a week since then. The last one we got was a week ago, today. He said that the defenses were holding, but that they could tell that the plague was passing swiftly through the country. Yer father wanted to know if he was to keep the south, or to join me here. I sent a message back saying that he should hold the south and protect our people.

He asked after you. We will send a messenger in the

morning with a guard, and hopefully get word back in a week or so. That is, of course, assuming the road south is travelable." His words were not encouraging, but there was still hope. Knowing that our fathers fought for the people in the south made us proud. We knew they would not leave unless they could bring the people with them.

It was later on in the evening when the king called his lords and war leaders before him. There were great men of Ireland there, legendary knights, and grizzled captains of men at arms. These men had fought before, and no doubt were itching to fight again soon.

The king began, "my lords. Our country has come under siege by the most dangerous enemy any of us have ever faced. My nephew, Prince Banion, and his loyal friends Sir Edward and Sir Sean have spent over a month traveling up through the south and western regions of our country. They have dealt with things that even we cannot imagine after the fall of Dublin."

At these words everyone in the room looked at us. It was if they were sizing us up. What they saw though, instead of boys, were three road hardened knights standing with weapons still at the ready. Many of the lords were dressed in finery and carried nothing but short knives that they would cut their meat with. The three of us, on the other hand, had calloused hands resting on the pommels of our weapons which hung below blood and dirt covered armor which we had not taken off let alone cleaned yet.

The king continued, "It is time, men. I'll not wait any

longer while the forces of evil take our land and kill our people. Turning them. Turning them into monsters that want nothing but to kill their fellow man. With the power of Christ, we shall vanquish these enemies and end this plague once and for all." At these words, many men said "amen" and crossed themselves.

The king then began to lay out his battle plans. We would leave the lord of Galway with two hundred men to protect the west and all the people seeking sanctuary there. We would then march east towards Dublin. After we retook Dublin, which would prove a formidable goal, the army would split in two. The king would head north and seek to reclaim all the northern counties, and I would lead the other half south to reclaim and hopefully reunite with my father. None of these experienced warriors questioned my appointment. They knew that my friends and I would know the land better than they, and that we were on a personal mission to rescue and protect our families.

Men years older and much more experienced in war bowed to me at this news. The king asked me to share our experiences with the undead so that these men could then tell their soldiers. We had to explain a new warfare. One in which the rules of battle had changed. We could not fight as if we were fighting normal men. I explained the need to crush or damage the heads of the creatures and how that was the only way to make sure they did not stand up again. We spoke of what weapons we had used, and how ranged weapons would still be valuable as long as the aim was true. The men listened intently, knowing that the words that I shared could mean the difference between life and death.

The king made one final proclamation after I had shared all that I could. He demanded that all the men in the tent have faced a creature and killed it with his own two hands before we left the following morning. He wanted them to be able to share the fear and experience with their followers so no one would be surprised at what we had to face when the enemy was in greater numbers. The king had rounded up many of the creatures as they wandered near Athenry over the previous weeks, and had them well guarded all day. At least half of the men in the room had not personally dealt with them yet, and they would be leaving and heading to that grisly business soon.

After answering some final questions, the king told us all that we would be leaving the following morning. It would take five days at least to get the entire army to Dublin and that was without anything stopping us on the road. Finally, the king asked for the loyalty of his lords. He declared that none of them have faced the numbers of such a strange enemy, and that we could not defeat it unless we stood together. Each of the men in the tent clasped the king's arm and then knelt to him before making their way out of the tent to ready their men to march.

The king looked to the four of us last as he placed his hand once again on Fang's head. We knelt before him but he commanded us all to stand. "You all have done a great service to Ireland already. You all deserve a rest. What say you?" He asked us all. We looked to one another and Edward spoke for us, "we will see it through to the end my lord."

I picked up after him, "We cannot stop until we have reunited with our families and Ireland is at peace again." Finally Sean said, "On our oaths as knights. We are with you my king." My uncle smiled and let out a booming laugh. "I didn't expect anything different. I bless you as knights of Ireland." He shook hands with Edward, Sean, and Reilly, and gave me a huge hug before telling us that we would ride with him the next morning. He then sent his steward to have servants come and clean our armor and give us fresh clothing. We headed off to wash, promising to meet Reilly back at the tent that the king had provided for us to sleep in near his. We knew that tomorrow would start a new chapter on our quest to rid Ireland of her undead foe.

CHAPTER 31

We did not want to wake up the following morning. It was the most comfort we had been able to sleep in for weeks. We could hear the sounds of the army packing and preparing to move outside our tent. The sound of horses running past told us that the scouts were leaving and we had better hurry. We rose, washed our faces in a basin of cold water, and found new clothes and our cleaned armor waiting for us.

The king had provided some light mail for Reilly along with a short polearm. It was like a spear, but shorter. It had a short thin blade attached to a three foot handle which we all realized would be perfect for the enemies we would face. We all dressed and put our armor on, strapping on our weapons. The steward came in at this point with a bound package. He told us it was a gift from his majesty for the coming battle. We unwrapped the package as the steward left, and inside were four blackthorn shillelaghs.

These shillelaghs were shortened to be only about three feet long. The nob on the top of the stick had been hollowed, and filled with molten lead making them heavier. These clubs were made for bashing in skulls. On the handle of each was carved our names and titles. Reilly's said "Reilly, Friend of Ireland." These were a rich gift, and not one that would compare to the normal shillelaghs that were used for walking or for general disputes. These were meant to kill. We found them easy to strap to the side of our horses' saddles, and they would be a perfect back up weapon in the coming battle. We were much pleased by this gift of gifts from the king.

The army gathered and then cheered as the lord of Galway took his two hundred men west to protect the people in what remained of civilized Ireland. There was not much ceremony past that. We knew our orders, and we left not long after they had. We rode to where the king was at the front of the column, and he was very pleased at our reaction to his gifts. I saw that he too had a shillelagh tied to his saddle as did many of the lords and knights around him. Our culture was beginning to take care of itself.

The vanguard of the army rode ahead of the rest of the host. They cleared out any creatures that were on the road before us. They also, for many days, scouted out the best places for the army to camp. We were moving very slowly as many men were on foot, and only knights or lords were on horseback. We passed a few villages and some outlying farms. Many we found abandoned without sign, and this worried us as to where the villagers had gone. Hopefully, they had made it into the protection of Galway before the plague had arrived.

We found some farms burned, and others destroyed as if they had been pulled down bit by bit. The struggles that these villages showed outraged the army and gave us reason to continue marching forward. We continued on determined to rid our country of this dire situation.

Destruction was not all that we saw as we headed east. We found survivors living in the hurried shelters that they had found most defensible. Some of these men joined us, others elected to stay where they were, and some decided to head west behind us into the safety of Galway.

This schedule continued for many days. We made it into County Kildare on the fifth day from Galway, and the king then called a day of rest. It was Sunday, and we knew that we could reach Dublin within a day or two. We did not know what to expect there, so the king sent scouts toward the city while the army rested. There were over a thousand men in the king's army. This was a large force, but we did not know the numbers of the undead we would be facing.

Some of the king's servants put up our tent for us, and we had lunch with the king that day. Messengers and scouts came and went as we sat with him, and we insisted that the king let us take a turn on the perimeter on guard duty. He argued that this was not a place for knights, and that the common soldiers would do a handsome job protecting the camp. Finally, I confessed for us.

"Uncle, we are bored. We have spent too many evenings sitting in a tent and after almost six weeks on the road, all of this waiting is making us stiff. We need to stretch our legs and get to know the men we will be fighting with."

The king smiled as he replied, "Nephew, you and your friends are wiser than your years. That is for sure. If you have recovered from your travels, and must have something to do, then I will give you an important job that will suit both of our needs."

He ended up tasking us with making rounds of all the guards, sentries, and incoming scouts that were in the area. This was perfect for us. The four of us and Fang were glad to get out of the bustling center of the camp and take to the trees in search of the sentries. The steward had made a map of the camp for us, which allowed us some direction when it came to who we were looking for and where they were.

We spent the next few hours working out the fatigue in our legs from sitting in the saddle for so many days straight. We checked in with all the sentries and the guards on both ends of the road coming into camp. We walked through the camp and were able to touch base with many of the captains and check on the men and their preparedness.

Reilly killed her first creatures as we made our way out to one of the sentries. Two of them came shambling towards us as we crossed a stream. She looked to us, and we motioned for her to take them. She would need the experience, and she had heard enough from us on how to fight them. She jabbed her poleax into the first creature's mouth as it opened it to bite her. She quickly withdrew the blade and, turning in a wide circle, met the second creature with a slash across the neck. They both fell to the ground lifeless, and we were all impressed with her natural ability with dealing with these monsters and even she looked a little shocked as she caught her breath and let her heart settle.

We later talked with some of the villagers who had

joined our army, and heard strange and unbelievable tales of what they and their fellows had had to deal with. Sometimes, a villager in the town had taken sick only to turn and begin to infect the rest of the locals before they knew what was happening. Sometimes, a single creature or even groups of them would come into the town and begin attacking those living there.

One man swore that two creatures had been dragged into the town center one night by a man on a horse, and they, being left there by the man, had gotten up and started biting those they could get within their reach. The one thing that was common across all the stories that we heard, is that people did not often know what they were dealing with before it was too late. There were only a few people who were able to figure out what was going on and protect their land.

Many became victims and thus new enemies for us. Even with the thought of taking back Dublin and in turn the bigger cities of the south, I knew that it would take months if not years for us to rid the entire country of the creatures, and even then, it could still easily come back with one that escaped our search, or one who came over on a ship like what seemed to have happened to several coastal cities in Ireland.

Fang took off that afternoon as we stood talking to one of the scouts as he returned from the south. He said that towards Wicklow, a village on a harbor on the coast, he had come across a large horde and had to turn back. It was with regret that he said that they turned and came after him. This was a threat the army would have to deal with after Dublin. We thanked him for stopping and sent him on to the king.

We went back to our tent at dinner time and ate and discussed what we had learned. There was a sense of anxious excitement in the camp. We all knew that, one on one, a creature fighting against a trained soldier wearing armor stood no chance, but if we were facing three, four, or five times as many creatures as soldiers we had in the army, then it would be a difficult, congested fight that we could not hope to win easily. This was just one city too. It seemed as if three fourths of our country was now in civil war against the one fourth still alive. The thought of these numbers sent us into silence which broke only as a herald came in and told us that the king had summoned us to council.

We arrived minutes later to see many of the other lords already in attendance. The king motioned for me to come to him, and I left Sean, Edward, and Reilly and went to his side. He took me by the shoulder and moved me to the back of the tent where we could have some privacy.

"Lad," he began. "It is much worse than we thought it would be. The two scouts are back from Dublin. Three more should be back and are not. We assume the worst for them. The city is overrun. I don't know if the people flocked towards Dublin assuming it would be a place of safety, but there are more creatures there than the city had inhabitants a month ago. We are facing near four thousand of them, Banion. Four thousand. That is at least four to one, and that is if that is all of them. That really doesn't count any of the beasts being in the surrounding country. You spoke to that scout; there is another big group to the south. What do you think? Can we take such numbers, or do we find a new strategy?"

I couldn't believe my ears. It seemed impossible for that many of the creatures to be in the city. Dublin was not that big after all. It was not like one of those big cities that I had heard of in the other countries of Europe. Like London in England with all its small cities and villages growing and merging into the bigger one, or Paris sitting in the middle of that large country, France. How could we possibly hope to defeat four thousand of the creatures?

As these thoughts raced through my head in seconds, another thought became more prevalent. The king was asking my opinion. I was sixteen and only a knight for a couple of months. Sure, I had been through a lot and seen much, but I did not think that this gave me enough foresight to prepare for a country-wide war. I was about to say as much when the king must have read my thoughts on my face. "Banion," He said, "You are family. Your da told me how you did in your trials. Don't doubt yourself. I trust you because you are kin. Tell me what you would council."

I thought for another minute, and then said "Uncle, we are at a disadvantage outside of the city. If they come on us in a great host out in the open, we will do well initially with our training and horses, but we will quickly grow tired where they will not. We have a disadvantage in the city too because they can come at us from all directions. However, if we split the army into four and instruct those pieces to split into smaller teams, then we can form shield walls and those in front with armor on their arms and legs can be replaced by the ones behind them when they become tired. That way no one is killed out of fatigue. We must remember also that any of our men that become bitten will become enemies themselves soon enough. We can't let another army raise itself up behind us from our own dead. Only in unity can we expect to survive such odds."

The king nodded his head at my words and patted my back. "I think that is the perfect plan, my boy." We rejoined the group and the king told the other lords what we were facing. There were shocked exclamations of protest at his words, and some of the lords preached the need to retreat. We all knew, however, that it could only get worse in this region if such a force was allowed to get bigger, and when the creatures in Dublin decided that they were ready to leave, then the rest of Ireland would fall without issue. It was here that the future of Ireland would be decided.

The king explained my plan to his lords and told them he thought this was the best way for us to fight in the city. We needed to fight through to the castle in case any of those left inside were still alive. If there were, we might expect as much as a hundred men reinforcing us if we could get that far inside the city.

The king broke up his force into fourths. He then set a commander over each of the pieces of the army and let them decide how they would break up their own forces for the assault. I saw much and learned much of how to be a leader of men from the king.

He had grouped the lords by region. This way, all the men fighting in each group would be fighting alongside the clans from the same area as them. This would give them courage and allow them to feel like they were fighting for their own lands and people in this fight.

The king then planned to have these four separate armies enter the city from the direction of their own lands as if we were protecting the lands from which they came. Edward, Reilly, Sean, and I would be attacking from the south. The king did not give me a command of one of the larger armies. He later told me this was because of my lack of experience, but also because my small team would be more effective following the major force from the south.

He wanted the four of us and Fang, who had returned during the council, to try to make it to the castle in any way possible and see if there were any left inside. This would hopefully be accomplished with a little bit of stealth as we assumed that the large armies would attract most of the undead to them which would allow the four of us to slide by unnoticed.

The king set the time for the attack at mid-morning the day after tomorrow. We would get into position around the city during the next day and kill any of the creatures that wandered near. We would then send in lighter men on quick horses to go into the edge of the city and to try and draw out as many of the creatures as we could. They would be much more defenseless if they were not bunched up, and were spread over the surrounding fields. Our knights on horseback would have very little trouble dispatching the creatures as the rode into the city on the front line.

The plan was for the four armies to try to take out as many of the creatures by stealth and with ranged weapons as we could. This making it as quiet as possible before we actually engaged them into combat. That would allow the initial shock of our knights on horseback to charge, get off their horses and send the horses back with their squires, and then form the first shield wall on the four major roads heading into the city. We would have twenty men across the front of the shield wall, and ten rows back. This left roughly fifty extra men in each army to guard the flanks and the back of the armies so that we could not be surprised and scattered by a few random creatures.

The plans were agreed upon, and they were all made very clear to all the commanders. They left and went to ready their troops and the king asked us to dine with him again that night. He said that he thought "It might be our last meal together after all so we should eat with friends and be merry."

The whole evening long, scouts and lords came to and fro from the king's tent with news of movements and questions on strategy. The king actually deferred to me and my friends on a couple of occasions since we were really the only ones in the whole army who had attacked a village and fought with different strategies. We had, after all, fought on horseback, on foot, together, and separate, with ranged weapons, melee, and even with our hands. We had been the first men in Ireland to ever face off against the creatures, and this, of course, had made us the first ones to survive an attack as well.

We said our goodbyes after the king had shown us a map of the city and our most likely and best route to the castle. He clasped my arm tightly and wished us luck the following day. He would be leading the army in from the west, and we would be heading south so we would not be together after midday. We went back to our tent, but were restless and could not get comfortable. We ended up sitting up until the wee hours of the morning discussing anything at all but the coming battle.

We were all anxious. Even when we had ridden in the village to fight off a whole large group of the creatures, there had not been more than thirty of them and the villagers had been helping us too. Our odds were much better. I laid down to try to get to sleep, but the only thought that was going through my mind was the memory of weeks before as the horde had overtaken us on the road, and they had swarmed the horses in a matter of minutes. That had only been about twenty creatures. Two days from now we would face as many as four thousand.

CHAPTER 32

We were up before the sun the next day. It had been a restless night and my nerves were bouncing as I pulled on my leathers and my armor on top of that. I put on leather gloves as well so that not much more of my body other than my face was visible. I hoped that the leather and mail would protect me against any arbitrary bites or scratches that might come my way the next morning. We would now officially be moving into enemy territory.

As soon as we left the camp we began coming across the creatures. Many chopped down with swords or axes as we rode past. The four of us used the time to practice with our new shillelaghs and get more comfortable with their weight, the amount of force required to swing them, and the feeling they gave as they smashed into skulls. They worked like a charm. Brains splattered as we rode past, and Sean began calling out his kills as we rode. "Four! Five! Six!" he yelled as we rode through a small group of creatures. They had barely turned towards us as we rode into them and they were little match for us and our armored horses.

Even Fang joined in as he would run ahead of us and heard the creatures into our path. He would nip at the creatures to get them to come after him and then he would run hard across our trail. As we dealt with the creatures, he would be up ahead leading the next in line to our merciless assault.

Early that afternoon, half of the army split away from the main host and turned south. We wished them all luck, and I raised my hand to my uncle as we turned away. He saluted me as he turned his own horse up the northern road. There was a little bit of trepidation in the fact that we were now in an army half the size of what we had been in. Before, in theory, we had been facing four to one odds. Now, however, if we had to face the city without help, we were at eight to one. I prayed as we rode that we would not have to face such odds.

We rode for a few hours in a very similar fashion as we had the twenty four hours before. We were regularly coming across creatures as we rode, but they were little match for our front riders who were well horsed, well armored, and well equipped to deal with groups of wandering undead. We did not ride hard because we did not want the horses to tire when we did not know what was up ahead, and we knew that they would need their full strength the next day.

At one point, we all alighted from our horses and walked them for a couple of hours. Many of the men in our part of the army were on foot anyway so it did us well to be seen struggling on as they did. We ate a small mid-afternoon meal to keep our energy up, and got back on our horses as the army split once again.

We had made it to the final split. One road headed northeast into the city, and half of our force of five hundred would march straight up it into the heart of Dublin city. The rest of us would continue on another hour and be able to come at the city straight from the south. We said our goodbyes to the lords and knights we had been riding with and wished them well.

It was with a much smaller force that we continued on to do our part to take back Ireland's city. The mathematics of how many of the enemy there now was in relation to our new group was frightening. I looked back over my shoulder at the other part of our army as we moved in opposite directions. Our plans were working just as we meant them to, but that did not give me any comfort.

CHAPTER 33

Three hours later and our entire army were in position on the road north into Dublin. We cleared the area and prepared defenses of our position in case the enemy came in the night. The scouts left not long after we arrived. We put wooden stakes in the ground all the way around the field that we had decided to make our staging area. They wouldn't really stop many creatures from coming into the camp if they really wanted to be there, but they would slow them down enough that it might make it possible for us to channel them into more agreeable kill zones.

The afternoon passed us by, and we became more and more restless as the sun sank and the stars began to shine. We knew there were would be very little sleep because of the close proximity of so many of the creatures. We were mere miles away from the city, and the wandering undead had already become quite the problem. We doubled and then redoubled the amount of sentries we placed around the camp.

My companions and I sat around the fire and talked wanting nothing more than the comfort of our friendship to be enough to remove our doubts and worries. Reilly seemed to be the most worried. She had never been or even seen a battle before and had only killed a few of the creatures over the last couple of days.

She had never been trained in battle or warfare, and we three had been trained since the moment we had the strength to hold a sword. She volunteered to dispatch any creature that came near to our area. I think she was doing this so that it would become easier when she didn't have the time to overthink her actions. Then was the time when it would come down to her or them, to life or death, to kill or be killed.

The four of us nodded off in turns around the fire. Fang's alertness made it possible for us to sleep much more than we would have because he would wake one of us if any of the creatures came anywhere close to us. He woke me a few times during the night and I had to get up and remove the threat. The creature's appearance in the dark caused me more fear than I would have ever imagined.

During one such an awakening, I rose to kill a creature that had come out of the forest near us. As I killed it and began to turn away, another creature came out of the brush and grabbed at me. I shouted and swung the heavy shillelagh around, bashing its skull. Fang was there in seconds, followed closely by Edward, Reilly, and Sean. It embarrassed me to think of how I had cried out over one such monster when thousands more were waiting for us the next morning.

We purposely slept in the next morning. The king wanted the four armies to lead simultaneous attacks at mid-morning, around 10 o'clock. We got up, said prayers when the priest came around to us, got dressed and helped each other into our armor, and lastly sat and sharpened our blades waiting for the signal from the southern army's general. The call came not long after this and we stood, hugged each other close, and remade our vow to one another this time including Reilly. "Together, or not at all," we declared and then mounted our horses and rode towards Dublin.

CHAPTER 34

We rode in silence towards our destiny and could practically hear the gears of fate's wheel turning as we followed the army up the road. I rode with Oíche drawn and in my hand. Our strategy of drawing out some of the creatures into the surrounding area had worked almost too well. Our group being well organized, it took very little effort to massacre those creatures that wandered too close to the army, or any that came onto our path. Occasionally, a lone man at arms would break ranks and step to the side of the road to exterminate any undead threats, and then he would rejoin the column as if nothing had happened.

We were getting used to this new life. We traveled fast. The anxiety of the entire army was almost palpable. The army almost had a shared consciousness where each man or woman in the group could feel the mounting tension as we drew near the city. As we reached mid-morning, the city came into sight. More importantly, our first glimpse of the city seemed to show the streets and buildings moving from the distance we were at. It looked as if a great number of ants were swarming all over the city.

A resounding cry came over the group as we realized that what looked like ants rushing to rebuild their fallen nest were actually thousands of the undead moving in sync with one another as they reacted to the coming threats.

Before the road dropped down off of the hill that we were looking down upon the city from, we noticed the glint of sunlight off of two other groups far off in the distance heading towards the city. It was a relief to know that we would not be dealing with the advancing tide of the undead all by ourselves. The other southern army, however, was not yet visible to us. We hoped they would be quickly with us in the city. We needed the plan to work perfectly.

We followed the road down from the hill and entered the lowlands to the south of the city. It was now that we brought the fight to Dublin. It was now or never. The dull moan of thousands of undead mouths was heard as our army let forth a barbaric howl as the men at arms shifted their shields in front of their bodies and drew their weapons.

A contingent of knights broke forth from the front of our army and road daringly forward to clear the path into the city as far as they could. Squires, also on horseback, followed closely behind them preparing to take their master's reins as these knights formed the first lines of our shield wall. From the back of our army, two groups of twenty five broke off heading both east and west. Their purpose was to protect the flanks of our approaching army, and then rejoin the back of the shield wall forming a rearguard.

In what seemed like only seconds, the crash of the knights and the ringing song of sword and axe were heard as the knights fell onto the enemy on the first street of Dublin. They hacked and slashed and made it almost all the way through to the main street before they were met by the congestion of thousands of reaching hands and gaping mouths intent on a meal.

We saw the shield wall forming and heard only one shriek from human tongue as the squires rode back behind the column and began picketing the horses in the field behind us. It would be their job, the thirty or so squires, to guard the horses against any unseen threats from outside of the city. If the worst happened, and it looked as if our two hundred and fifty men were losing, they would join the shield wall to die with a sword in their hands.

A select few of the younger squires had been tasked with watching the battle from atop a mill that stood on the river in the southern country surrounding the city. If our armies were to fail, they would ride with great speed back to Galway so that some in Ireland would know of our bravery, our story, and our fate.

Time seemed to speed by as we too entered the outlying streets and buildings of Dublin's south quarter. Small battle groups of ten men moved off from our main host to clear the streets perpendicular to the road we were on so that we would, for the most part, only have to face an enemy from the front. They then rejoined the main battle group. With cries of "Ireland!" and "Éire!" and "Good King Patrick!" our force linked up with the knights in the front of the shield wall and not a moment too soon.

Only one knight had fallen to the creatures in the ten minutes it had taken for us to reach their wall. He had twisted his ankle getting off of his horse and dropped hard in his armor. The shield wall had not yet formed, and so he was instantly seized by dozens of hands as they pounded and tore at his body with dirty and broken fingernails.

He would have been fine for a few minutes as he was in full armor, but one creature had worked a finger into the gap beneath his helm and ripped it off. The scream we heard was the knight upon realizing that he was doomed. It had taken more than a score of the creatures to finally defeat him, but it was the weight of his armor that actually cost him his life.

The knights were standing strong as the undead rushed towards them. They were keeping time with a warrior's chant and most importantly keeping the right side of their shields locked into place with the left side of the shield to their right. These men were not facing weapon carrying warriors, so the second row did not need to spend their energy holding their own shields over the heads of those on the front line. They jabbed with spears and long swords over the shoulders of their fellows and helped stem the tide of undead foe.

There was already a low wall of bodies in front of the shield wall, and the knights, upon realizing that their backs were now secure with our arrival, began to push forward. It was dangerous to step over many bodies because of the potential to trip and fall, but judging by the quickness with which they pushed forward, it showed their extreme discipline and sword craft. The dead knight had been pulled behind the lines and our army started moving forward.

The creatures in the city now recognized our presence, and they came forward in droves for their turn to try to bash and smash their way past our shields to get at our bodies. The pressure of hundreds of the creatures on the first line became apparent as many of the knights on the first line sheathed their swords and used two arms to hold their shields in place. The men behind them became the killers.

At once, a grizzled leader of men at arms, Johnny Mac as he was called, commanded the knights to kneel. This was a dangerous move, but the overwhelming burden on the pushing hands was likely to break the wall. The undead felt no pain, so they felt no fear. Hundreds were now packed into the street opposing us. The knights on the front knelt, and this allowed the men in the second row to easily slash and hack the enemy over their heads.

The four of us watched for many minutes and saw how well we were doing, but, even as the bodies stacked up in front of us, it did not seem like we were making any progress. Whenever a soldier dropped one of the creatures, five took its place. We knew this was not going to be easy, but we also knew that this wall was not our job.

I sent Fang to scout out one of the side roads that would connect to one of the roads paralleling our own. He came back and gave us a bark, and we turned our horses up the side street with one last glance back at the wall. Two large creatures had pulled down two of the shields and the knights behind them and were banging on them with their fists. It took only a matter of seconds, but, even as these knights were dragged back by their fellows and the man in the second row took their place, we could see the blood pouring out from under their helmets.

The unity and discipline displayed by the men was encouraging. Our concern was lifted, but we also knew that there was much more danger in what we were about to do than what our army had to deal with.

We slipped quietly away with Fang in the lead. Our ranged weapons were out, and we stealthily took down any creatures that happened upon us as we headed deeper into the city. I shot arrow after arrow and these arrows were accompanied by the zip of Edward's sling and the whoosh of the bolts shot from the crossbow that Sean carried. We could hear the sounds of battle from streets over and the crash and ching of sword and axe on flesh carried with it.

The moans of the undead seemed to be unending and only grew louder. From what we did not know. Eventually, after the neigh of one of the horses had attracted a handful of creatures, we had to dismount and continue on foot. We slapped the backs of our horses and were glad to see them run back the way we had come. We hoped that they would leave the city and the squires could catch them rather than them becoming food to the merciless undead.

Our first big shock was upon reaching the middle of Dublin. The river passed through the middle of the city, and there we found hundreds of the undead milling about. It was obvious that the thousands who had probably been occupying this area mere hours before had then gone off in all directions chasing the sounds that the armies were making to draw them to their deaths.

Despite our plans working rather well, we had not anticipated that many of the creatures would not take after the sounds preferring the mindless inaction of waiting for a meal to come within reach. We had to cross the bridge and continue up the road on the other side to get to the castle.

We did not know how to do this without attracting all the creatures in the area. One at a time, we could take on such numbers, but a hundred versus four and a wolf were not good odds. Fang sniffed around the end of the street where it emptied into the square and he let out a short and rather quiet "ruff" and disappeared around the corner. We knew to trust his instincts, and so we followed him not knowing what was around the corner.

We tried to muffle the sounds of our weapons and armor as we followed Fang down the side of the river bank. We continued to shoot at the creatures whenever we knew we could hit them in the head. The castle came into sight as we moved over a much smaller bridge across the river. I left my bow, and Sean left his crossbow there at the other side of the bridge. We had run out of arrows and bolts, and we could not let our bodies become encumbered by their weight or the bulkiness of strapping them on our backs.

Oíche sang as I tore through the undead that rushed us as we crossed the bridge. I could hear the dull thump of Sean's hammer as he brought it crashing down on his enemies. The grunts of Edward as he bashed with his shield or swung his axe made it clear that he too was defeating his enemies. Even Reilly seemed to be holding her own after a glance showed me that she was fighting with the poleaxe in one hand, and the shillelagh in the other. She spun on her foot like a dancer and stabbed, poked, and bashed at her enemies and they fell before her as if she had been training at war her whole life.

We all got caught up in the rush of battle to notice that we were attracting much more attention than we should have. I was dragged from my revelry as Fang barked loudly and I heard Sean yell my name. "Banion! Come on! They're surrounding you!"

I looked around me and noticed that I had moved away from the group in my effort to feed Oíche's insatiable hunger for undead flesh. I cried back, "go! I'm coming!" and hacked my way towards my friends. We ran up the main street towards the castle which was clearly in our view at this point. Many of our enemies followed after us as we went, and it became difficult as the weariness of battle slowly began to ebb away our strength.

Abruptly, I heard Reilly scream ahead of me as I saw reaching hands from a doorway grab hold of her hair as she passed and drag her screaming to the ground. Edward threw his axe through the doorway and I heard a dull smack as it landed hopefully on Reilly's attacker. She was screaming, "Not today! I'll not go today!" and was kicking and hitting with all of her strength as the groping hands continued to painfully pull at her hair. I chopped down hard cutting through all of her outstretched hair and felt Oíche's blade bite into the ground.

I helped her to her feet and turned to see Edward, weaponless, beating back three creatures with only his shield. He had not had the time to pull his shillelagh from his back and continued hitting them even as Sean, waylaid by five creatures himself, tried to reach him. Reilly stooped for her weapons and called out a hurried "thanks" as we both rushed towards our friends. We were able to neutralize the closest creatures and give Edward enough time to draw another weapon.

There was little time to get to where we were going and so we continued on as quickly as we could. A surprise came when we rounded the corner and stood facing hundreds of the creatures with their backs turned to us. We had come upon where the northern army had plunged deep into the city. We could hear them yell and scream as they fought on against their tireless enemy.

Sean turned to us as we all tried to catch our breath. "We must help them. They seem to be losing more men by the second," he implored us. It was true; the army facing us seemed to be less than half the size it should have been. We could see how they had come to a bad spot for such a battle. They had come to a space where three roads met, and were thus fighting their battles on three fronts.

We put our heads together and whispered hurriedly. "We cannot leave our mission to the castle." Edward started. "It is our only job in this fight. If we find it abandoned, then we can come back."

I added, "Edward is right. The castle is our only purpose right now. We must get there." Sean conceded with a pang of guilt obvious on his face and we continued on as the castle began to loom up ahead of us.

Fatigue was beginning to set in as the rush of battle slowly ebbed. My armor seemed to weigh a thousand pounds, and, as I looked towards my friends, I realized how ragged we all seemed. Reilly had a great rip on the back of her leather armor and above that her hair was extremely short on the back. I would have laughed at her new boyish appearance, but she probably would have stabbed me. There were scratches and cuts all over Edward and Sean's' armor. We were all covered in gore, and Fang was almost unrecognizable as he had been right in the heart of all the battles that had taken us to where we were.

We heard a loud cheer in the distance, but did not know what that meant. We started to cross the wet ground surrounding the simple moat around the castle and were stunned to see it full to the brim with the undead. We made it to the gate as another cheer echoed behind us. There were no sentries visible on the parapet, and so Sean began to bang on the door with the haft of his dented and scratched hammer. Edward, Reilly, and I all formed a semicircle around Sean to protect his back.

Sean after getting no response for many minutes started to break through the wood of the door with his hammer. No sign of life was a really bad thing, and it seemed near impossible to be quiet while trying to break down a gate with a hammer. The creatures came at us in pairs and trios from the surrounding parts of the city. We could not see very far past us, but could see the road back to the river that was choked with the undead. "Sean!" Reilly pled. "Hurry! There are more coming than we can take by ourselves!"

She was right of course. There were scores of the undead stumbling and even crawling towards us at the castle. The creatures in the moat had begun climbing over one another in an effort to reach up towards us. Finally a loud crack came from behind us, and another swiftly followed it. We quickly assassinated any creatures within reach, and Edward used his last stones to kill a few with his sling. With a great grunt and a whoosh of air, Sean pushed open the gates of the castle's outer keep.

The sight that met us caused me the greatest fear I have ever experienced in my life. I glanced over my shoulder and saw past Sean the reaching and waiting arms of dozens of undead women and children. The castle had been overrun. We backed away from the castle with as much haste as we could manage and they followed us. Hundreds of the undead were stalking us from inside the castle walls, and we had just let them out.

We were backing towards the river when another horde came stumbling out of the side street where we had seen the northern army before. We were trapped in between two large groups. It seemed like this was the end of all of our journeys. We began to pray out loud together as we looked for any out at all. Fang began to howl as he too must have realized our dire circumstances. Sean lifted Reilly onto the thatch of the nearest building, and, after helping Fang up the same way, the three of us climbed up to await or at least postpone our fate.

CHAPTER 35

Just as the two hordes began to merge into one large group right in front of us, the source of the earlier cheers was discovered. From the road nearest to us emerged the rag-tag group of survivors of one of the northern armies. They were less than fifty men, but they came in with the ferocity of a thousand. They crashed into the enemy in front of them, and gave us the slightest hope. There were still hundreds of creatures around us, and our situation would have seemed even more dismal had not the king's army as well as the remnants of the two southern armies become visible around where the road we were on opened up to the main square near the river. They came crashing, hollering, and hooting with glee at our apparent victory over the undead army.

We stood with renewed spirit and began to cut, stab, and hack at any of the creatures that ventured near to the roof we were on. As our merging armies attracted the attention of many of the undead, the focus left us and we were able to drop back to the ground and join the assault. We watched the great heroics of the knights and men at arms that were struggling against the current of our enemy.

Sean ran ahead as we reached our comrades and yelled with great triumph as he squashed the heads of any creature that was unfortunate enough to come into his path. He laughed as he swung his hammer, a merciless tune adding to the din of battle. The men around him gave him a wide berth, but had their own spirits rise to fight alongside him.

Edward and Fang were dancing to and fro as they bashed their way through to the rest of the army. Edward killed just as many of the creatures with his shield as he did with the shillelagh in his hand. Whenever he would find himself absent of an enemy to kill, he would beat the shillelagh against his shield and attract more of the creatures to their deaths.

In harmony, Reilly and I cut into our foes. We followed the paths of Sean and Edward and cut down any stragglers that managed to escape the fury of our friends. First I was on the left and then Reilly as we switched places. Reilly laughed as she stabbed forward with her poleax. She used the shillelagh in her off hand to separate pairs of the undead to manage them more easily.

Oíche sang her own song as I swung her. I knew my arms were tired and would switch hands on occasion, but I did not feel the fatigue. All I knew was that we were close to victory and I only needed to continue on for a little while longer. As we fought, the amount of creatures we faced slowly lessened. We were coming to the end of this first battle for Ireland's freedom.

Our whole army now numbered little more than five hundred men when it had started hours before at over a thousand. These few hundred slammed into the remaining undead in the center of the city, and we were all rejoined as the separate armies came up parallel. The king rode up on his horse covered in gore from head to toe. He beamed at me and shouted in victory as I clasped his hand. It was hours later as the sun was headed down when the fighting truly started to slow.

CHAPTER 36

There were still undead within the city, but their numbers were dwindling quickly. The king had reestablished himself in the inner keep of the castle after we discovered that it had been held against the plague and had many survivors. The entire castle had not fallen. The armies reunited and we put stout guards on all roads to and from the city. There were roving bands of men on horseback with torches that were scouring the city for any enemy to be found lingering after our hard fought victory. It would take weeks to fully reclaim the city from our enemy. A street by street, and building by building search would have to take place, and new walls would have to be put up.

The king called us into his presence before we had even found a time to eat something or wash the grime off of our bodies. We had led a group of knights to St. Patrick's Cathedral and had cleansed that holy place so that we would have a place to praise God for our great victory on this day.

The king was rather morose as we walked into his great room. He began with an exhausted and unsatisfied look on his face, "Banion. What you four accomplished is beyond all understanding. You should have retreated when you saw that the square was held against you, but you went on anyway. The streets, my streets, are filled with the blood of our enemy, but this was not but the first of many battles that we will have to reclaim our kingdom. You must head south as soon as you all have recovered from the battle. I have already sent messengers back to Galway, but we must plan for the extermination of this plague from our entire country."

An overwhelming realization came back to me as he mentioned me going south soon. I had forgotten the plight of our fathers, and the uncertainty of their fate and the fate of my home and people. The king continued, "Ireland owes you more than she can repay you for all that you boys have done, and you too Reilly. And Fang!" He spat as Fang nipped at his hand. "You shall all be rewarded with land when we have enough time to breathe and get the country's affairs in order. At the very least, let me congratulate you all and tell you at the very least that I raise the three of you knights to the rank of Lord. This is the least I can do in such circumstances that we are in, and for the service you have given me. You have honored your fathers and your king. Reilly, your sacrifice too has been great. When we take back our country, you too will be rewarded greatly."

We were shocked. There had not been a man our age given a lordship ever. This was more than a title. The king's gift promised us all land in Ireland, and would allow us all to be leaders of men to war and the defense of our great country. We knelt before him and thanked him for his generosity and magnanimity. He smiled, raised us to our feet, and embraced us all.

As his stewards and messengers came up and demanded his attention, the four of us and Fang left and went to find food and water to wash off the filth of battle.

We clapped one another on the back, and smiled for what seemed like the first time in weeks. We relived the events of the day and realized how lucky and how blessed we had been to make it through to the end. It seems that all of us had had multiple occasions when we might have lost our lives. We stopped by some of the resting men from the other armies and heard amazing stories of chaos, death, and destiny. Our forces had been reduced to a fourth of its original size, and yet we had accomplished something huge. Each man seemed to know that this was just the beginning of the much bigger fight for Ireland's independence, but it was good to bask in this first of victories.

Reilly left us not long after to go find someone to cut off the rest of her hair. She said she wouldn't trust a man's touch to such a job so she went in search of one of the camp wives. We found a spot on the parapet overlooking the river, and built a fire. A steward found us and brought us water and food and new clothes.

Sean had collapsed by the fire and had fallen asleep inside his armor. Edward had gone off in search of his thrown axe and had taken a few men at arms with him. Fang was gnawing on a sheep's bone near the fire. I began to strip off my armor and couldn't help but notice how stained and broken it all seemed to be.

I thought of what my father would say if he saw my equipment looking thus. A tear came to my eye and I knew that I would find him no matter what I had to do to get back to him. I looked down at the blood on my hands and knew that there was much more to come.

EPILOGUE

It was the better part of a week before the king finally declared Dublin free of the enemy. Since the battle, men at arms and knights alike had been hard at work building the defenses. We used the buildings of the city and the river as walls. Some buildings were torn down and used to block up streets. It was as if we were rebuilding the city to never have to face such a calamity again.

The main streets were all turned and hedged so that any wandering hordes that made their way towards the city could not run all the way through without a fight. Lofts were built in the buildings so that men could sleep above ground and not worry about waking up to find a creature at their feet. Watchtowers were built at regular intervals so that all of the surrounding countryside could be watched and warning could be had by all.

Three days after our victory a large horde had come from the west. It must have been the group that had followed the scout back towards the main army days before. We were ready for such a threat at that point. The army had been separated into three groups that were each tasked to be armed and armored for battle for a third of the day. With the watchtowers going up, the horde had been spotted and our army waiting for them in the field outside of the city before they even had a chance to come inside.

The four of us rode out in the battle and helped where we could. We had become somewhat of local heroes for fighting our way alone to the castle during the assault. The men in the army fought with renewed strength as we entered on horseback yelling our battle cries as we came. The battle lasted barely an hour as the army had become quite used to fighting together and our strategy was improving.

The king called us before him on Sunday. He had reclaimed his throne but was busy with the preparations for what he called "the rest of the war." Messengers and scouts had been sent out the day before to all the major cities to discover what they could of the fate of the country.

The king looked tired as he smiled when we entered the room. He spoke, "knights, and lady." Reilly stirred a little as he called her a lady. He continued, "We have struck a blow to the enemy, but you know as well as I that this is only the beginning."

I knew what was coming and I felt both fear and elation. "You must head south once again. We must know the fate of your fathers and know if the southern kingdom still stands against the undead." He prayed for us and wished us well. He would be taking half of the army north by the end of the month with the hope of liberating the counties as he worked his way into the northern kingdom.

We would be leaving the next morning to head south once again. He gave us sealed messages to my father, and even some for the English king. We did not know if we would ever see each other again, and he wanted Ireland and the king in England to know our story and our hope even if he was not able to send word himself. His desire was that, no matter how long it took, that we would make our way to England if the southern kingdom was saved and find out if that kingdom still fought against the undead.

Our last decision together was for me to give up the command of the army heading south. My desire was to travel with stealth and help any along the way that we could. A week after we left, the army would come after us and we would operate as scouts for that army. We would be able to travel much more swiftly and find out the state that the southern kingdom was in without attracting too much attention. This way we could best lead our revenge against the undead plague.

It was a big decision that Sean, Edward, Reilly, and I made to travel alone once again. There might have been more safety in numbers, but we were going home. I looked around at my friends and knew that this was just the beginning.

49562436R00123

Made in the USA
Lexington, KY
10 February 2016